AFRICAN COWBOY

LIVING DREAMS

PHILIP PHIL-EBOSIE

Mira Publishing House CIC,
PO BOX 312
Leeds LS16 0FN
West Yorkshire
England
www.MiraPublishing.com

African Cowboy. Living Dreams

By Philip Phil-Ebosie
ISBN: 978-1-908509-04-8
First published in Great Britain 2013 by Mira Publishing
House CIC.

Typesetting by www.genietags.com
Printed and bound by Book Empire – Harrogate - UK

A full CIP record for this book is available from
the British Library.
A full CIP record for this book is available from
the Library of Congress.

Mira Intelligent Read

CHAPTER ONE

Clint could not make up his mind which style to pose. He shifted his leg imitating Hugh O'Brian in "Wyatt Earp." He had placed his hands in front of his belt, tucked his forefingers in between the belt and his shirt and lifted his right leg onto the stone support of the flowerbed. The heels of his cowboy boots kept slipping off the stone. He decided to settle for Karl Malden's pose in "One Eyed Jacks." The stone pillar provided a good back support but he always felt the trick was in the eyes. Kimosabi had said, "Regard everyone as the enemy. Touch your guns when necessary. Look them straight in the eyes."

The football match was scheduled to start by 4pm. The gates had opened by 12 noon. It was now 2 o'clock and the stadium was almost full. This was an old stadium. It had been built during the colonial period. It was part of the old college built by the Church Mission Society. The church had since closed down and the college was now dilapidated. The fence and pillars had been part of the wall surrounding the school and protecting it from intruders. The wall itself had also broken down in places. This made it necessary to have security stop people passing through the holes in order to avoid paying gate fee. Clint looked at the crowd and felt the gates would soon be closed. The gang was on guard duty to keep the crowd in order. They wore their full cowboy outfits for the day. The rest of the gang was spread out at strategic points around the stadium. Although Clint did not smoke he had his short thin cigar in his mouth the way he had seen Clint Eastwood do it. When anybody looked at him he would twirl it in his mouth for effect. He did not light it. If he really wanted to look tough he would look at the person and spit on the ground. They always moved away after that. He had thrown his small blanket over his shoulders. Not because he was cold but that was the way Clint Eastwood did it. His wide brimmed hat protected him from the noonday sun. They had been doing this for some years now, keeping guard duty at the stadium during football matches, athletics championships and any other event. Clint was bored with the whole set up. This feeling of boredom had been building up for some weeks. He had tried to discuss it with Roy Rogers many times but Rogers did not understand. Roy Rogers was the nearest Clint had to a best friend.

Clint was basically a loner. For some time now he had felt he was wasting his life, doing the same things over and over, day in day out. He dreamt of being out on the range; chasing cattle, driving them through the prairie come rain or shine, sleeping out under his blanket at night while looking out for cattle rustlers or rattle snakes. He counted the years he had been with the gang and felt he had nothing to show for it. Sometimes he thought of his life before the cowboys and decided he did not want to go back to that either. His remaining relations did not ask for him and he never went to ask for them.

They had treated him badly and saw him as a nuisance and a liability. Clint felt it was time to move on. Yes he had heard it said many times in cowboy films, it was time to move on. The urge was eating deep into his fiber. After today he thought, yes after today. Clint felt he could not continue playing cowboys any longer. When they leave the stadium they would go to Central Hotel to rouse up the place.

Clint looked up. Roy Rogers was two pillars away leaning against the wall trying to disguise his handicapped leg. That was his "Bronco Lane" pose. He didn't like to be called "Chester" after the limping assistant to Matt Dillon in "Gun Smoke." He chose Roy Rogers as his name because the real Roy Rogers could sing and play the guitar. Further down from Roy Rogers was Dan Blocker towering above everybody at 6ft 8ins. He took his name after Dan Blocker of "Bonanza" fame. He was always sweating. He always wore a waistcoat and a scarf in the hot sun. The afternoon sun was beating down hard. Clint felt Dan must do something about his weight even though Dan was somebody to have when fights broke out with other gangs. In the old days people used to be afraid to fight with the cowboys. Not any more. They knew the guns they wore were not real and they thought the gang looked funny in their cowboy outfits. Clint could sense them laughing at him. It was this knowledge that the cowboys were not real that depressed him. He had made up his mind to give up this pretence of playing at cowboys. He had come to feel the

3

Fulani nomads, known as the Fulani cattle pushers were the real cowboys. They pushed the cattle on foot, driving them down south, through towns and villages to the big city markets. They trained them, branded them and reared them. All the things real cowboys did. Rogers did not understand.

Clint had argued, "How can we be cowboys without cattle or horses?"

But Rogers did not see it like that. Clint had decided that yes, after today he would find his way out. After today he would stop this pretence of playing cowboys. He wanted to experience the real thing. He had been thinking of going up north to join the Fulani cattle pushers. They would push cattle together from the North to Lagos. The cattle pushers were just a day's train ride from here. He will take the train up to Kafanchan. First he had to collect his money. That thought made him a bit anxious since he was sure Kimosabi would make trouble for him. They would not allow him to leave easily or peacefully. Clint was so deep in his thoughts he did not see the gang coming.

Kimosabi walked up to Clint and nodded towards the stadium office. This was the sign that the gates had closed. The rest of the gang were behind him. They were to go and collect their money. Seeing Kimosabi and the gang depressed Clint further. This pretence had eaten deep into their lives. The way they walked, the way they used American cowboy slang. Even the way they sat on chairs. He felt more determined

4

now. He would definitely leave the gang. It had been a hard decision for Clint to make. He had been thinking of it for a long time. Now he had to do it. The gang had been his life.

Clint stepped into the line with the others. They walked cowboy style with slow measured steps towards the stadium office. As he walked behind the others Clint remembered they used to be ten in number. Now they were only seven. He looked at Tonto, Billy the kid and Cassidy with their dirty clothes and old worn shoes. He looked at Kimosabi. Kimosabi was so much older than they were. He must be nearing 40 years. No, he thought, he had to go now. The gang had come together 7 years ago. Kimosabi was the natural leader. He had brought the idea to form the gang. They had agreed to save money for the fancy clothes to be worn on the Christmas Day carnival. The carnival parade would go around their town Igandu. The best dressed group would win a prize. They had decided to dress like cowboys. They chose the name "The Cowboys" for the gang. "The Cowboys" all chose names from the numerous cowboy films they had watched over the years. In those days most youths were found in cinema houses.

There was a new cowboy film showing every week, three times a day. They were in the cinema house from morning till night. Most times they didn't think about eating or going home. They spent all their money on the films. There was nothing else to do in Igandu town. The youths and their gangs knew all the cowboy films and the dialogues almost word for word. The fun was to say the words with the actor in the film. They shouted encouragement to the actors. They cheered the heroes and booed the villains until the final show down. Fights often broke out in the cinema hall to coincide with the fights on the screen. Kimosabi and his boys sometimes came out of the cinema bruised and battered. Unlike in the films, they were throwing real punches. Clint had chosen his name after Clint Eastwood in "Fist Full of Dollars." They had all stopped using their real names. Clint's real name was Ahmed Sukro. His adopted name had pushed it far into the background. He had no cause to use it again. Chukwudi became Roy Rogers. Kasumu Edu adopted the name Cassidy from "Hopalong Cassidy." He argued that the two names Kasumu and Cassidy were similar. The film "The Lone Ranger" was shown repeatedly in the cinema houses around the town. Musa Isa as Cassidy's right hand man naturally became "Tonto." In the film "The Lone Ranger," Tonto called "The Lone Ranger" Kimosabi. Nobody in the gang had known the meaning. The gang agreed that "Sabi" which in Pidgin English means to know, when joined to "Kimo" which must mean Master, would give you Kimosabi. This must mean "The Master that knows all." Titus Zachary dropped his real name to become Kimosabi. Ola Kareem the youngest in the group and the fastest on the draw took up the name "Billy the Kid."

Clint was fifteen then. He was homeless like most of the other youths. They used the money

6

they made on guard duty to feed themselves. At other times they did odd jobs to survive more especially jobs that enabled them to live their fantasy. Most other times they did any other jobs they could find. They emptied dustbins or swept rubbish off the roads. They cleared blocked drainages and dug gutters. Sometimes they would go to restaurants and beg to wash plates, other times they would cut grass where possible or bricklaying for people who could not afford to employ professionals. With their cowboy clothes they were easily noticed anywhere they went. They would help people to carry heavy loads or anything that would earn them money. Once in a while they would provide security, escorting money on foot for a trader to the bank. They called that "Hitting pay dirt" and of course they did security. Whatever money they made would be put in a central kitty. Kimosabi managed their affairs.

Kimosabi had given them shelter and organized their lives. When they could, they would sleep in the cinema houses. If they were lucky, they slept where they were on guard duty. Sometimes they slept in Kimosabi's place. They had named it "The Ponderosa" after the ranch in "Bonanza" and because of Dan Blocker who stayed with Kimosabi. The place did not have any resemblance to the Television Ponderosa. Kimosabi lived in one room in what is known as a "Face me I Face you" building. A house with five single rooms on the left side and five single rooms on the right hand side. The bungalow had three small shower rooms and two smaller rooms used as kitchen at the back of the house. These amenities were shared by all the occupants of the single rooms. The Cowboys slept on old torn mattresses on the floor of the room. On a cool evening they slept outside on the verandah of the compound. The neighbors sometimes grumbled at the amount of people squatting with Kimosabi but they were too afraid to speak. Dan Blocker made sure of that. Although the Landlord did not live in the house Kimosabi was on good terms with him. Kimosabi had helped out the landlord with odd requests on many occasions.

CHAPTER TWO

The Office Manager looked up to see a bunch of cowboys by his door. Kimosabi was leaning against the wall twirling his gun around his finger. The manager understood the game and enjoyed playing along with them.

"Oh yeah, you guys have finished. How much was it we said?"

He received a hard cold stare from The Cowboys. They always felt their stare could frighten anybody. The Manager took out some bundles of money from his desk and threw it on the table. He knew The Cowboys liked it when he did that. Kimosabi put his gun away, checked the bundles and stared hard at the Manager. He leaned against the wall and answered with his best American accent.

"Mister this ain't right."

The Manager took out some more money and handed it over to Kimosabi. He had kept the exact amount in his desk. "It's complete now."

Kimosabi nodded to his boys signaling that they should leave. He handed the money to Dan Blocker to put away and said as a parting shot,

"We'll be back."

He knew of course that they would be back for the following Saturday's football match. The boys allowed Kimosabi to go to the front. He added the special swagger to his walk. He got this from Jim Brown in "100 Rifles." He always did this when the gang got paid. Each member of the gang would also walk with a swagger. They strolled down the street, holding up the traffic while they crossed the road. People stared at them and some tried to avoid them. Clint turned to Rogers.

"Where are we going?"

"To Central Hotel," replied Rogers.

Clint drew back forcing Rogers to limp into step beside him. He wanted them to talk without the others overhearing. He shook his head sideways.

"I am tired of all this, man. Look, we can't keep pretending. We are no cowboys."

"Yeah..." replied Rogers absentmindedly.

He had heard Clint's argument so many times before.

"The Fulani cattle pushers are the real cowboys. I have been thinking about it seriously. I want to go and join them."

"You can't join them. You know nothing about cattle," replied Rogers.

Rogers was not fully convinced that Clint was serious and it showed in his voice and his reply.

"Kimosabi will not let you go," he added.

"We will see, my mind is made up," continued Clint.

"How can you join them? You will sleep on the grass. Man look, it's a tough life out there."

"That's what I mean. Their life is just like real cowboys," said Clint looking into the distance.

From the stadium road they took a short cut through the village looking footpath heading to the Hotel. Clint wondered if he would miss the town when he leaves.

Although Igandu was called a town it still had the appearance of a village. Most of the houses in the town were bungalows and some still had thatched roofs. People fetched water from public pumps which were situated on some major parts of the town. The three major highlights of the town were the stadium, the cinema hall known as Rex Cinema and the Central Hotel. The Central Hotel was a one-story building. Upstairs was used for paying guests but most of the rooms were occupied by prostitutes. The Cowboys chose the Central Hotel because the setting always reminded them of the hotel in "Gun Smoke" run by Marshall Dillon's girlfriend Kate. Clint came out of his thoughts and for a moment felt disoriented. They walked into Central Hotel. The Central Hotel was built more than 40 years ago. It opened day and night. The inside was well lit with colored lights to give that nightclub feeling during the day. The dilapidated walls were covered with posters. The Hotel also served as a whorehouse. A woman known to everybody as Mummy ran it. There was a live Congolese band that played the afternoon shift. The hotel was full and people were dancing on the dance floor. The Cowboys strolled over to their favorite table and took their seats. Kimosabi placed his feet on the table cowboy style. Their routine was well known to the clientele.

"Tonto get the drinks," he ordered.

Clint and the others also took their seats. Their entry into the hotel had already made the impression they wanted. Everybody had taken notice. Clint's mind was again far away. He was calculating on what he was going to do. He knew his action could lead into a fight. A fight between him and Kimosabi would be one sided. He could only rely on Rogers to take sides with him. Kimosabi may want to put up a show for the hotel clients. Clint swore to himself that it would not be at his expense. The fat madam strolled over to greet them. She knew they would have been paid. It was Saturday and a match day. The madam was dressed as usual in her long oversized gown. She was popular and jovial to everybody. She often flirted with Kimosabi. The only time she was unfriendly was when they owed her money. Her favorite clients were those that got drunk and spent a lot of money. Mummy was not married but she had a boyfriend. He was a short man who always sat in the corner away from the bar and to the left of the back door. He would sit there drinking and looking half drunk. Sometimes some clients would buy him a drink. He never said a word but was completely under Mummy's control. Mummy placed one hand on her hips and looked straight at Kimosabi.

"Kimosabi how's business?" she asked.

"Give us food, the usual," he replied, still putting on his tough act.

The usual meant beans porridge. The type they had seen cowboys eating with wooden spoons.

"You boys are in money today. You can also pay your debts" Mummy said.

She didn't smile as she wanted them to know she meant business. Tonto put two bottles of locally made gin on the table. He attempted to slide the short glasses on the table across to Kimosabi but the first two keeled over. He shrugged and passed a bottle and a glass over. The others reached across and took their glasses. Kimosabi took the bottle and removed the cork with his teeth conscious that eyes were on him. He poured a shot of gin for himself and gulped it down. He then passed the bottle down to Dan Blocker who took a swig from the mouth of the bottle and also passed it on to the next man. Dan Blocker wiped his mouth with the back of his shirtsleeve. One of the hotel's serving girls came over to sit with Kimosabi. Kimosabi liked to pose with the girl sitting on his knee cowboy style.

Clint felt this was the time to act before everybody settled down. There was no point prolonging what would amount to a show down. He swallowed two shots of the gin for Dutch courage and put his feet up on the table. Kimosabi and others looked at him. Clint knew only Kimosabi was allowed to put his feet on the table. He pushed the bottle towards Rogers and stood up with his hands on his belt, Clint Walker style in "Cheyenne."

"Kimosabi, I want my share from the stadium money. I want to leave."

All the others stopped what they were doing and looked at Clint with surprise. Kimosabi pretended he did not hear and turned to Dan Blocker.

"See what he wants."

Kimosabi did not know what to think. Was Clint serious? Did he really want to leave or was he just acting up. He didn't like the look of things.

Clint steeled himself for any eventuality. He knew he could not just walk out like that. He needed some money for the train ride too. It was now or never. Dan Blocker stood up slowly with his eyes fixed on Clint. Dan and everybody else knew that in a straight fight Clint did not stand a chance. This was the moment Clint had been dreading. He reached across the table and grabbed the gin bottle again. Dan Blocker made to move forward but stopped when Clint cracked the bottled hard against the edge of the table, pointing the broken jagged edge towards any of them that dared to come forward. All the gang stood up except Kimosabi. The music stopped. The dancing stopped and all eyes stared at their table. Kimosabi slowly pushed the girl away from him. He stood up, the way he had seen Charles Bronson do it and placed his legs apart with his hands resting on his guns. Some of the crowd who thought the guns were real started to move apart. Some moved towards the pillars murmuring that Mummy should do something.

Dan Blocker turned to Kimosabi.

"Shall I kill him now?"

He got that line from John Wayne's "Stagecoach." He always used it when he wanted to frighten the enemy. The Madam pushed her way through the crowd to their table. She was even angrier now.

"If you guys make trouble here tonight, you will pay for the damage. I mean it," she said.

Kimosabi saw that all eyes were on him. Some of the looks were hostile. A voice shouted from

14

the crowd.

"Throw them out."

He stared at Clint for what seemed like ages, looked round the crowd and decided to sit down. He collected the bag of money from Dan Blocker's side, took out some notes and threw it on the table towards Clint.

"Naa let him go," he said as he relaxed back in his chair.

Clint picked up his money with his left hand and stuffed it into his jeans. He stepped backwards away from the table, turned and started to make his way through the crowd. They stepped aside to let him pass. The rest of the gang looked at Kimosabi for a sign but he motioned them to sit down. Clint dropped the broken bottle by the door.

"He will be back," Kimosabi said to no one in particular.

Roy Rogers did not look at the others. He knew he must talk to Clint and at least give him some elements of support. Clint was his best friend. He got up and limped after Clint. He wanted to talk to him to find out if he was really going and at least to say goodbye. Dan Blocker made a move to go after them but Kimosabi put a restraining hand on him. He shook his head and told him to leave them, that Clint would be back.

The music started again and the dancers moved back on the dance floor. Kimosabi took two glasses and poured a shot of gin for himself and one for Dan Blocker. They both adjusted their hats and leaned back on their seats. The hotel girl came back to clean the table and collect the broken pieces of bottle. They hardly noticed her. Their thoughts were still on Clint. Although Kimosabi still believed that Clint would be back he did not understand what really happened. He had always liked Clint. He felt Clint could always be relied on. In the old days he would have beaten Clint for what he did. Things must be changing. They must be getting old he thought. Kimosabi was surprised that he had taken this rebellion by Clint so lightly. His reaction had been to diffuse the tension. But this was a bad example to the others. Clint had called his bluff and he had done nothing about it. Yes, they must be getting old. Times must be changing. Lately he too had been thinking of his life too. But what else could he do. This was the only life he knew. Real cowboys don't give up. They don't even die in their beds. They die on their feet. The more he thought about it the more he admired Clint for his courage. Not just for standing up to him but for having the guts to make a break for it. Time will tell if he would come back. Kimosabi hoped he would. They were family. He wondered why he never got any hint that Clint was planning to leave. He remembered that Clint had been moody lately. Kimosabi glanced down the table and silently counted the cowboys. They were getting smaller in number every day. The Cowboys was his life. What would he do if they broke up? Dan Blocker turned to look at him. Kimosabi nodded his head towards the bottle. Dan Blocker poured both of them a full shot each. Kimosabi took a swig from the glass and then knocked down the remainder immediately. He gave a sigh nodding his head up and down as he felt the effect of the drink run down his body.

CHAPTER THREE

Clint was outside leaning against the wall with his head back and his eyes closed. He was taking in gulps of fresh air. Rogers moved closer.

"Will you be back?" asked Rogers.

"Naa" answered Clint.

"Does that mean you are going up to Kafanchan as you said before?"

Clint nodded and opened his eyes. Roy Rogers noticed they were moist. Clint moved off from the wall. They walked towards the high street. Rogers continued to ply Clint for some answers.

"What will you do there?"

"I will wait till the cattle pushers pass the town then I'll join them."

"How will you do that?"

Rogers had the ability to make Clint frustrated with all the questions he normally asked. Rogers did not always understand the answers easily. Clint snapped at him.

"Look what's all these questions about? I will talk to Dan Fulani; I have told you that before."

Dan Fulani was the name given to all cattle pushers.

"Then I will wait for the next cattle driver."

They walked in silence for some time.

"How are you for money?" asked Rogers. He wanted to help his friend.

"I have some savings," answered Clint.

"When are you leaving Igandu?" asked Rogers.

"I have told you before. I am leaving today."

"How do you know the Kafanchan train comes

today?"

"I have already checked. When I collect my things I am going to the market to catch the truck to Sabonji. The train will be there at the crossing in the evening."

"Are you sure you can make it?"

"I will try, I will."

"These trains breakdown on the road and sometimes you may have to spend some days on the track waiting for the relief train."

"That's no problem. I am ready for any eventuality."

"You know you will get into Kafanchan at night?"

"Yes I know."

"Where will you stay?"

"Rogers, don't make things any more difficult for me. Don't worry I will be ok."

Rogers put his hands in his pocket, brought out some money and offered it to Clint.

"No man, don't worry I have enough. I will be ok."

"Please take it. I want you to take it."

Clint stretched his hand and took the money.

"Thanks."

Rogers wondered if he would see Clint again. They had been close buddies in the gang. Rogers shook his head. He felt he had to explain himself.

"I can't leave the gang Clint. It's all I have. Where would a one-legged man go? I can't beg on the streets. The Cowboys made me somebody. People notice me. Some fear me. Girls want to be with me. I have some money in my pocket. Most importantly, I eat and sleep well. I have friends and family. That's what the gang means to me."

Clint listened to everything Rogers had said. He could understand his feelings. They walked down the high street turning off towards the house where Clint rented one room.

"The gang has been family to all of us," answered Clint. "But times are changing. We must move on to the next phase of life. You must be able to know when one phase has ended. Don't stand still otherwise it's just a matter of time. Before you know it, the world has passed you by. Look at all these people around you, we are part of them and we are not different. We are getting old, Rogers. We can't play cowboys into old age."

He had said these words to himself over and over in his mind. Clint playfully slapped Rogers on the back and continued talking.

"Where is your real sense of adventure? That was what the real cowboys had. That's what we are losing. We are standing still man. I don't expect you to understand but it's something you feel. I feel it. It's a very strong urge and until it's satisfied, I will remain restless."

This was what he had been trying to tell Rogers all the time. Rogers for the first time felt he understood Clint.

"I wish I could come with you."

"Naa, its okay," answered Clint.

They stopped walking. There was nothing more to be said.

"I have to go back," said Rogers.

"I know."

Rogers brought out his hands. They shook hands.

"Take care," he said.

"You are a true cowboy man," Clint answered trying to make Rogers not feel too bad.

"You too" said Rogers, "Look if you need any help anytime don't hesitate."

He turned and started limping back to Central Hotel. Clint watched him go. Rogers had always stood by him. He felt he would miss Rogers more than anybody else in the gang. Rogers took their fantasy too seriously. They had a lot of good times together, putting fear into people in those days, especially with their guns. They could catch some of the local girls who admired their hip American cowboy slang.

Rogers kept his face straight heading towards the Hotel. He did not want Clint to see the tears running down his face and besides cowboys did not cry. This was one of the most painful days of his life. He had hoped that what Clint had been saying about leaving, was not true. He had not wanted to believe it. He had not had many close friends in life. Rogers felt most people ran away from making friends with him because he was handicapped. He swore to himself. If he had more courage he would have gone with Clint. He cursed his parents for giving him one leg.

The leg, which had been cut off when he was an infant so that he would grow up to be a one-legged beggar. From the proceeds the family would feed. He had been a beggar until the day he smuggled himself into the cinema hall to watch a cowboy film. That film was "Gunsmoke." He saw Marshal Dillon and his deputy, Chester. The film changed his life. He used to meet the others in the cinema and slowly they became friends. Once in a while they would give him money. His father had died leading a mob during a religious uprising. The father was accidentally shot by the Police. His mother had run away. The rumor was that she left with a man. Rogers had continued begging until that day in the cinema. That was also his first time of sleeping in the cinema. The second happiest day of his life was when they formed "The Cowboys."

Roy Rogers remembered how he had gone back to begging for a short while to raise the money for his Cowboy clothes. The Chester in "Gunsmoke" did not really have any cowboy clothes. He only wore his shirt, trousers and boots. The real Roy Rogers had an elaborate outfit. This was what he saw in the films and why he had taken the name Roy Rogers. He prayed he would meet Clint again.

Clint turned and headed for his room. There was really nothing to pack. He needed to collect his savings, which were hidden under the floorboard and to take his extra pair of jeans and cowboy shirt. These were all he had in the world. That's the life of a cowboy he always told himself. Cowboys always travelled light. When he left the room all he could think of was the gang. He pictured them in his mind. He was surely going to miss them. Yes, he would be back one day to see them, to see Kimosabi, tall and thin, with his leather jacket and trousers. His outfit was made from imitation leather normally used to make upholstery. He also kept his moustache, razor thin. He was kind to a fault. Always ready to help anyone in distress, more especially members of the gang. Many of the children in the town idolized him.

Clint could not remember when last Kimosabi lost a fight. But he had had to do what he did. That was the only way to leave the gang. Kimosabi did not like people leaving. Maybe indirectly he was afraid of the gang breaking up. Looking back, Clint reasoned no one had left as easily as he did. Dan Blocker was the second in charge in the gang. This was due to his size. You had to pass him before you could get to fight Kimosabi. Dan was different from his hero in Bonanza in many ways. The real Dan Blocker was a gentle giant. This one had a mean streak in him. Clint was happy he did not have to tangle with him today. There was a time they almost became close but Clint did not easily understand him. Dan Blocker's real name was Isa Aten. Clint believed that Dan thought he was too soft. He also believed that in spite of what Dan always said about his home, that he came from the Benue plateau area. Clint smiled to himself when he remembered Cassidy. He was always unshaven, dirty and carrying a small bottle of whisky in his pocket. He was a brave, short man with a funny sense of humor. Always making the gang laugh but never shirking in a fight. He could always be relied upon.

There was no train station at Igandu town.

There was a stretch of land about two hours journey from Igandu where the train always came to a stop for about ten minutes. Anyone who wanted to travel used the opportunity to jump on the train at that point. Most people who jumped on the train either hung by the sides or climbed on top of the train and sat down for the ride. The only way to get to that stretch of land was to hitch a ride on one of the trucks taking foodstuffs, fruits and vegetables, to Sabonji town. At the stretch of land where the road crosses the rail track one would jump down.

Clint made his way to the other side of the town to the market. It was an emotional walk for him since he felt he was taking a last look at the town, at least for some time. He had kept the idea of this journey a secret for a long time. Since he did not have many friends outside of the Cowboys there was no need for him to go to see or say goodbye to anybody. Clint took in the sights and the smell of the town. All told, he was not sorry to be leaving.

It was already early evening by the time Clint got to the market. Luckily there was a truck fully loaded with tomatoes, plantains, bananas, and onions ready to leave for Sabonji. The bus was almost broken in two and leaning on one side. Clint was not worried because most of the trucks plying that route were in no better condition but they always managed to reach their destination. Clint walked over to the truck, haggled with the driver and soon came to an agreement on the fare. He paid his money, climbed on the back of

24

the truck and waited for the market women to make room for him in the cramped sitting bench. There were four women already seated. Two of them were fat and took up most of the seat. The women could not understand the funny-looking young man climbing into the truck, with funny clothes and rained abuses on the truck driver. They complained that the truck was a small truck and that the driver should get moving. The women wanted him to get moving so that they could get to Sabonji to unload their market before darkness and also to prevent the driver from taking another passenger. Clint noticed the effect his gun was having on the old women and removed the belt and the holstered gun. He put it in his bag. The women relaxed a little. Clint squeezed in between them, then put his bag on his lap, lowered his cap and closed his eyes. To his surprise the trucks engine kicked the first time and they were off. Clint felt elated. His adventure had started. Within a short time Clint had fallen asleep. He had felt tired. It had been a long day but he was happy.

It was as if there was an alarm clock in his brain, as Clint woke up just as the truck was approaching the railway crossing. The driver stopped and shouted at Clint to come down. Clint jumped down, stretched himself and looked around the desolate land mass. He noticed a cluster of people grouped together a short distance away and figured that was where the train stopped. The driver started the truck and answered Clint's question by pointing to the group of people as he drove off. Clint strolled towards the group. This was going to be his first train ride and he looked forward to it with anticipation. Cowboys sometimes rode on trains. He had seen it in countless cowboy films. The last time was in a Van Heflin film. Clint saw Van Heflin as a villain. He was always a villain in the films. Clint looked around the rail track. The people must have been waiting a long time for the train. They were looking restless. Some children were running around the tracks. Some adults had placed mats on the ground and were sleeping. Others stood around discussing while a few sat under the shade of some trees. One man was eating. Clint's entrance had caused a little stir. The people just stared at him. He overheard someone say that the train would soon come. Clint moved away to stand, alone by a tree not far from the group. He did not want to talk to anybody. There was only one place the train went to and that was to Kafanchan. He wanted to be left alone with his thoughts and hoped the train would arrive soon. Clint took out his gun and belt.

He wore his gun to put fear into the people and to make sure he was left alone. Like many adults and youths in Igandu, Clint had never felt like taking a train ride before. Even just for the hell of it. He knew some cowboy films had trains but they were going from one cowboy town to another. Igandu was the only town that had cowboys. Train rides were for people going somewhere. The gang had nowhere else to go. Clint thought about the gang. None of the gang had ever ridden on trains. They had never had cause to leave the center of Igandu town and therefore never really discussed it. Igandu had been all they knew.

Clint looked down the rail line and wished the train would come. He was a little impatient to be on his way. He felt a little scared but excited. He now wondered what the train would look like close up. His thoughts went to Kafanchan. He wondered what the town looked like. He had thought of this day, time and time again. Suddenly doubts started to creep into his mind. He did not know what he was going to see over there. He had had many sleepless nights thinking of this day and journey. It had taken him time to take that decision. Now that he had taken the step he decided he had to see it through. Even though he knew nobody in Kafanchan, somehow he just had the feeling things would work out fine. He knew it was part of his character to take spontaneous action. He often took decisions on the spur of the moment and saw it through. There was no way he would give up now.

Clint's mind went back to when he had run away from his uncle. His parents had sent him to his uncle to apprentice and to learn a trade. It had been a hard decision to take, but once he had made up his mind to run away he didn't think twice, he just did it. Clint was to learn to sell old car parts at the mechanic village. It was called the mechanic village because the local government had allocated those plots of land for car mechanics, to ply their trade repairing

27

old second hand cars and trucks. The business was not a lucrative one and his uncle, who was a trader, did not hesitate to whip him with the cane everyday he came home from work. Clint did not have to do anything wrong to receive the whipping. To make matters worse he had to go without food most of the time. Not because there was no food but his uncle regarded it as punishment for imaginary misdemeanors. He believed the cane was the only way for learning. The man was naturally wicked Clint thought. He was always fault finding. Clint still had the cane stripes on his back to remind him of those days. He had been eight years old when it started and went on until he was fifteen. That was when he decided to run away. That day he had left at night and walked till morning not really knowing where he was going. He had a little money in his pocket. In the morning he had found himself at Akpokena village. There he bargained with the lorry driver to carry him to anywhere his money could take him. They had crossed Iburu River and traveled the whole day until he ended up at Igandu. He knew his uncle lived at Ibado but he was not sure where his parents were or lived. Clint suspected he had been sold to the man he called his uncle since the man never raised the issue of his parents. He did not even know the man's full name and all he could remember of his parents was that he called his father Da and his mother Ma. Now Igandu was all he knew. He had been at Igandu for seven years and had never wanted to go back to Ibado. He vaguely remembered the journey from the house to Igandu but all he knew was that he spent two nights on the road. The day he arrived at Igandu he had slept at the motor park. In the morning he washed plates for the woman who cooked food at the motor park. In return she gave him food to eat. He did this for some time until the day Kimosabi came to the motor park playing the guitar and singing. Then his name was Ette. He wore traditional clothes. Clint liked him immediately and they had become friends.

One day, for the first time, he was given an off day. He went to the cinema with Ette. It was his first time in a cinema. He loved the film. It was "Aloma of the South Seas." That day he slept at Ette's house. The next day they went again to the cinema. The film had been changed. This time he watched "Sinbad the sailor" and he was hooked. He went to the cinema every day. From then on Ette had shown him how to smuggle himself into Rex Cinema without paying. A few months after, they formed the Cowboys. Clint thought to himself that yes he had made it with the gang. He was a cowboy. Now he wanted to be a real cowboy. He had suffered before and made it. He was going to make it now. The sound of the train in the distance woke him from his daydream.

CHAPTER FOUR

Alhaji Tijani was putting the final touches before leaving on his journey. This was the moment he had been waiting for. The last cattle push before he handed over his business to his eldest son Ibrahim. It was a dream come true. He wanted to relive the life of a cattle pusher, to sleep under the moonlight and enjoy the solitude. It was the culmination of a lifetime's work. This was how he had started in life, as a Fulani cattle pusher. Now he was a successful cattle dealer with hundreds of cattle in his ranch. He also had a thriving "Trailers for Hire" business. He dealt in animal hides and leather. Through his contacts, he handled government contracts. He was now a successful businessman with a house in Lagos, Kano, and Kafanchan.

Alhaji Tijani had never forgotten where he came from. How he had started. He was just a small boy, a young Dan Fulani. He was never tired of telling his family his story. Alhaji had made a promise to himself that whenever he retired, he would undertake one more cattle push from Kafanchan to Lagos. He would do it the old way. Not like nowadays when they just put cattle on the trailers and transport them to Lagos. The only concession he gave to the family was that he would join the trailer at the head bridge at Okuta. He felt there were no challenges anymore. The youths of nowadays were too soft. They had no sense of adventure. No sense of achievement. His wife Fati was crying and being comforted by their daughters Aminatu and Hauwa. She had tried all in her power to dissuade her husband from embarking on the journey. He was now seventy-four but still agile for his age. He looked younger and felt younger than he really was. Alhaji Tijani had always been very stubborn. Fati had enlisted the help of her children to try to stop him. She tried to convince him that the journey was too dangerous nowadays. She had quarreled, she had argued, she had fought in her own way but Alhaji would not hear of it. She reminded him that people were preparing for Durbar in the town of Igara and that the Emir would expect him there. That nobody would push cattle today. He explained that the roads would be free for him. Alhaji felt he would have passed Igara town by the time the Durbar was starting. And now the moment had come. She feared for his safety. There were robbers on the roads. There were also more cars and lorries too. The roads would be too busy. Ibrahim and his brother Dauda had already accepted the situation. They knew their father and knew he would not change his mind. Aminatu and Hauwa his daughters would go along with whatever their father said, more especially Aminatu who was their father's favorite. The other workers were standing around pretending they had not noticed the drama. Ibrahim came up to his father.

"Pa everything is ready."

They were standing around the gate waiting for the signal to let the cattle out. Fati looked at her husband once again.

"Tijani are you still going through with this?"

Alhaji ignored the question and made a big show of counting the cattle one more time.

"Tijani at least take more money with you."

"I don't need more money. I did it before with less. Ibrahim, open the gate," he ordered.

"At least let one of the boys come with you," said Fati.

Alhaji knew he had to leave or the crying would start again.

"Woman, go back to the house! We have been over all this before. Ibrahim open the gate."

Ibrahim opened the gate. He knew this was not the time to disobey his father.

Alhaji Tijani tapped the lead cattle gently on its hide.

"Hey Jana hey," he shouted.

The cattle made its way to the front. The herd moved off on the first step of their journey to Lagos. Alhaji turned to his youngest son Dauda.

"Dauda, you and Ibrahim make sure there will be a trailer waiting for me at the head bridge at Okuta."

Then he turned to his wife.

"I will see you in Lagos."

"Hey Jana hey," he shouted at the cattle.

Alhaji followed the cattle from behind. Fati cried even louder but her children restrained her. The herd had already gone quite a distance when she opened her eyes to see her beloved husband with his cattle herding stick on his shoulders and his arms resting casually on the two ends of the stick.

"May Allah go with you," she whispered.

Alhaji knew that the most difficult part of the cattle push was the first day. If things were to go wrong on the first day, then a lot of bad luck would follow all along the trail. He had decided to take it easy on the first day. The most important thing was to get started. He needed to leave the family or he would never leave. All the fussing and pleading by Fati was getting to him. He knew he would miss her but he felt she should have remembered about when he was a cattle pusher. That was when he had met her. He would push the cattle just a few miles to the small town of Igara. There he would sleep the night. He planned to stay by the open fields near the place where the Durbar would take place. He would leave before the Durbar starts. Starting this way would give him a chance to get into his stride and also to get the cattle in the right frame of mind. He needed to get a good night's rest because he had not slept well lately. He had been thinking about the push and all the arrangements that went with it.

"Hey Jana hey!"

This was a momentous day for him. It was almost harder than his first day as a cattle pusher. Alhaji pushed all doubts about his ability from his mind. He knew he would make it. He felt good. Alhaji was tall and straight backed for his age. He was practically bald but had grey hairs on the side of his head. He always shaved clean every two weeks. He was feeling emotional now as he put the cattle in their stride. Alhaji had come a long way as a poor boy that was destined to beg, steal and commit all types of crimes into adulthood. Life had not held much future for him. He was already roaming the streets with all the other homeless, jobless youths that were ready to do anything for pay, including murder. He remembered how politicians would employ them for little money. They would give them food and alcohol. They provided them with Indian hemp to charge them up and to get them to commit mayhem in the town. This destabilized their political enemies. It did not bother them if innocent people died in the process. That life had been suffocating for him. He knew the way he was going would lead him to a tragic end. He longed for freedom.

It was the freedom which the Fulani represented to him. They always looked relaxed. Their needs looked very few and they were at peace with their environment. They traveled for miles, visiting city upon city, town upon town. Alhaji Tijani had longed for such freedom. He remembered how he had gone to the cattle market asking how he could become a cattle pusher and if possible join one. It took time until fate smiled at him. One of the small boys learning the trade did not turn up and the Fulani pusher, impatient to get going since he had a deadline to keep, gave the young Alhaji the chance to push with him. He did not even have time to go home to tell his people. They left immediately and here he was today.

"Hey Jana Hey," he shouted, louder than he had intended.

The excitement and emotion were stuck in

his throat. Alhaji Tijani guided the cattle out of the front stalls and the market gate, through the streets and on to the main road leading to Igara. He checked that his bag was secured on his shoulder. This was for his blankets, food, medicines and other odds and ends. He touched inside his long shirt to make sure his sword was well secured. The small dagger too was well secured in his belt. Over his shoulder were his bow and poisoned arrows. All these were for his self-defense. On his neck and upper arm he wore his amulets for spiritual protection and across his shoulder was his stick for controlling the cattle. Yes Alhaji Tijani felt he was ready for his last cattle push. He could not be more ready than now.

CHAPTER FIVE

The train to Kafanchan was already late. Clint walked further away from the crowd to stand by a clump of trees. The passengers too had been trying to avoid the cowboy figure leaning against the tree with his hat pulled down over his eyes. They did not know what to make of the young man with the funny clothes, wearing the gun around his waist. Clint could not be bothered. He knew the effect the cowboy clothes had on people. This had been the whole reason for joining the cowboys. His mind went back to Central Hotel. He had been going over what happened there. He knew his leaving would definitely affect the gang. He had not been the first to leave the gang he reasoned. His mind went to Billy the kid. Clint had a soft spot for him. Billy the kid was the youngest in the gang. Clint wondered what would become of him. He was still a young boy. Just a year older than Clint was when Clint joined the Cowboys. He was stubborn and troublesome like his hero in the films. He was just over sixteen years of age and small for his age. You could easily mistake him for fourteen years. His mother had left their home and got married to another man. She had left Billy the kid with his father. The boy whose real name is Ola Kareem, was maltreated by his stepmother. His father was unemployed and had sold most of their property to support his drinking habit. He and his wife beat Billy almost on a daily basis while the stepmother did everything to drive Billy out of the house. Since she was the breadwinner, Billy's father did everything his wife told him so long as he got money from her to buy the local Gin. Due to the amount of housework Billy had to do in the house he was always late for classes. He invariably got caned and put in the corner facing the wall of the classroom by the teacher. In no time he was thrown out of school.

One day he ran away from home. Nobody looked for him although he had been hiding very near the house. After a few days he wandered back to the house exhausted and hungry. His stepmother threw him right out of the house telling him to go back to the gutter where he crawled out from. She rained abuses on Billy and his mother while Billy's father slept soundly in a drunken stupor. Billy never went back again. Clint remembered he used to follow the Cowboys around. He practically worshipped Kimosabi and Dan Blocker. It soon began to look as if he was part of the gang since he was always with them. After sometime, he graduated to going on errands for the gang until one day the gang voted unanimously to induct him as a member. When he made enough money from his share of guard duty he bought himself his outfit and his guns. He always wore black and soon proved that he had the talent to draw very fast with his hands. Billy the kid was the only one that wore two guns in the gang.

Clint's thoughts were disturbed by the sound of the train in the distance. Excitement built up inside him. He moved a few steps away and watched the train as it started to emit smoke and slowly engaged the brakes until it passed him. He was surprised how big it was close up. He tried to keep pace with his eyes on the wagon coaches as they sped past him. The train finally came to a stop. The noise from the brakes put a little fear into Clint. People started rushing to jump on to the train. Some hung by the sides, others hung by the back of the train. Some others climbed on to the roof of the train where they sat down. Very few went in through the door. Clint found himself standing towards the back end of the train. He noticed that he was still acting like a cowboy. It was the way he had lifted himself onto the train, cowboy style. He was posing "Randolph Scott" style. He hung at the corner of the back of the train. The train waited. There was complete silence as the train stood almost in the middle of nowhere. The signal signs changed and the train started to move slowly. Clint hung on tight as the train picked up speed. Clint used his right hand to pull his hat down tighter on his head to make sure the wind did not blow it away. When the hat was secured, he adjusted his shoulder blanket to make sure it too was secured. The fear and nervousness of his first train ride slowly left Clint as he allowed himself to enjoy the ride.

Clint noticed that to his left was a door with a small platform. He maneuvered his way slowly to the platform. He stood there and watched the surrounding landscape speed past his vision. He felt he had now started to live the life of the real cowboys. He was well on his way. He remembered he had seen cowboys walk on the roof of the train. He wasn't sure if he saw it in the film "Have Gun will travel" but decided he was not yet skilled enough to try it. He tried the handle of the back coach and the door opened. He looked down the corridor. The corridor was blocked with people. Children were running everywhere. The train was jam packed. Clint looked further down the corridor. He could make out that other coaches had doors at their back too. Eyes turned to look at him as he stepped inside the coach. He closed the door and picked his way through the mass of people careful not to tread on some legs. There were travelers going to the market in Kafanchan for their goods. Clint made his way towards the other end of the train. The further he went, the less people were in the corridor and the coaches. Clint passed some empty coaches and decided to go and sit inside. The train picked up a fair speed and was rocking from side to side. . . Clint was enjoying the sound of the train. At the speed they were going he judged they would get into Kafanchan well into the night. He hoped that the train would not break down as people had told him they often did and Roy Rogers had confirmed. A day or two on the tracks would only try his patience and cause him an unnecessary delay while waiting for a relief train to come to take them. The train did look old and rusty.

Clint looked at his reflection in the window glass. He liked the way he looked. He looked tough. He remembered that the trader that sold the cowboy outfits used to travel by train to

Kaduna. He bought the clothes there. Till today, one still had to go to places like Kaduna to buy the outfits. With so many traders now traveling up and down the country, it was much easier to order them than in the early days, he reasoned. The traders often bought the clothes and guns at some of the big markets around the country. Sometimes the outfits were sewn in Igandu town. Once one could buy the materials, the tailors would attempt to sew it. They would need to have the right descriptions and specifications. They would need to be guided throughout the sewing.

Clint opened the window to allow some fresh air into the compartment. He did not hear the door open. He felt a hand touch his belt lightly. He turned around. He was surprised to see a little boy standing half in awe and half afraid. Clint did not want to disappoint him. He put on his mean "Tuko" look and spat out of the window.

"Git," he said.

He got that look from Eli Wallach in "The Good, The Bad and The Ugly." The little boy ran away.

Clint sat down, adjusted his hat and closed his eyes. He had mastered how to be half-awake and half-asleep, "Glen Ford" style. The only other person to come into the wagon was the ticket collector. Now he understood why people hung on the sides or sat on the roof. These were people who did not have tickets and were just hitching a ride. Clint smiled to himself. Yes they too were living the life of the cowboy. The collector did not find it funny. He wasn't afraid of Clint and his outfit. He had been to many cities and seen many things. He was used to people trying to sit in the wagons without paying for their ticket. He told Clint to either produce his ticket or pay for one otherwise he would be thrown out of the train. Clint brought out money to calm the collector. They settled on how much Clint should pay. He collected Clint's money but did not give Clint a ticket. Clint knew the money would go into the collector's pocket and would not be reported at Kafanchan. With that out of his mind he now relaxed in his seat to enjoy the ride.

The train sped along, passing the little towns and villages. It passed the little hamlets of the Fulani dotted all along the route. Once in a while some passengers would try to enter the compartment but one look at the lone passenger who sat there and they would double back to find another compartment. Clint knew that the further they went north, the more of an oddity he would become. He looked out of the window. He began to notice the sparse vegetation of the terrain and knew they were well on the way to Kafanchan. He was finally on his way to join a Fulani cattle push and to live the life of a real cowboy. It occurred to him that he had not really given much thought to what he would do when he finally got to Lagos. Would he become a cattle pusher or would he stay in Lagos? He did not know. Would he go back and join the gang again? No, he had made up his mind that he would not pretend again. He would find time to visit his old pals again whenever he could but he would never join them as part of the cowboys again. Clint found that no matter how much he tried to block the gang out of his mind, they still kept wandering back to his consciousness, more especially Rogers and Kimosabi.

Kimosabi cut a dashing figure in his outfit which he modeled against Gene Autrey, his first cowboy hero. Kimosabi could play the guitar, sing, and ride a horse. In the early days when the Cowboys had just started, he would lead them in the front, riding a white horse, which he had hired for the day. He would play the guitar and sing while they followed on foot behind him. The horse was called "Champion" after the horse in the film "Champion the Wonder Horse." All the children from the neighborhoods would tag along at a safe distance from the group. The Cowboys would go from street to street and people would give them money and gifts. The girls would be admiring them, more especially Kimosabi. Those were the good old days. The gang did not do that anymore.

There was a time when Kimosabi was the best known man among the youths. That was when the festival was the biggest known festival in Igandu. It was held annually in the town. Apart from the Cowboys there were two other gangs in the town. The Boma boys and the Supermen. The Supermen dressed like Superman and were led by Shazam, while the Boma Boys were reputed to be the toughest. Their bands accompanied both groups. To join the Boma Boys you had to be able to withstand being whipped by all the members of the gang. The new initiate would stand in the middle of the group, with his body bare from the waist up, to bc whipped with dried horsetail whips. Some of the members inserted pieces of razor blades in to the whips before they were dried to ensure that the whips would cut whoever was being whipped.

When the Boma Boys walked round the town accompanied by their band of drummers and flutists, the sight was something to behold. Their rhythm was irresistible. The members and spectators would always have the urge to dance. When the music moves any of the members, the member would jump into the middle of the group to be whipped on his bare arms and legs. This was done to show that Boma Boys were tough and brave. Many a time a spectator watching the members whipping themselves, without flinching, would jump into the middle of the group. He would soon jump out again after receiving some strokes on his arms and legs. This provided added entertainment for the crowd. The Boma Boys used to pull the biggest crowd in the town. They had their followers and the Cowboys had theirs. Often fights would erupt between their supporters. They would argue which group was the toughest. Of course the Cowboys were helped along by the cinema and the image of cowboys as the toughest breed of men in the world.

Cassidy had once jumped into the midst of the Boma Boys and stayed there. The Boma Boys whipped him more than they had ever whipped anybody. Cassidy did not move or flinch. After some time he started to dance to their rhythm to the delight of the crowd. Some days later when the leader of the Boma Boys tangled with Dan Blocker, he was knocked out and the myth of the Cowboys as the toughest and roughest gang in the town grew. The gang had nursed Cassidy's cuts and swellings for weeks after the whipping incident. The gang gave him everything he wanted. He had made them very proud to be Cowboys. From that day Cassidy commanded a special respect within the gang. It was that act of bravery that made Tonto to pull nearer to him. They became the best of friends.

Clint soon fell asleep. He dreamt in his sleep. He felt disturbed. He could see the gang in his dream. The noise from the train did not help. He slept for about three hours. When he awoke, the train was pulling into Kafanchan. It had been a long ride. He was hungry. He looked for his bag. It was still there. Night had come but the station was well lit with electricity. Clint got up and decided to go out of the train from the opposite side of the platform. He had jumped down before he realized what he was doing. He was still playing cowboys in his mind's eye. The train started pulling away and he relived the scene with Charles Bronson in "Once Upon a Time in the West." He remembered how the train had pulled away to reveal an empty platform. For an instant, Clint expected to see Woody Strode, and then he came back to reality again. He was only acting out his fantasy. He realized he was still on his way to join the Fulani cattle drive to Lagos. He had to find somewhere to eat, look around the town and find a place to bed until the morning.

CHAPTER SIX

Alhaji Tijani had woken up by 5:30am in the morning. He had his bath by a small stream on the outskirts of the town. He said his morning prayers. He took the dry meat and some bread that his wife had packed for him out of his shoulder pouch. After eating he called out to the herd. Some of them were already up and standing. Others lay on their tummy grazing. The herd responded slowly. Rising to the call and prompting by Alhaji Tijani, they started to move in an acceptable orderly procession. Alhaji Tijani wanted an early start so that he would have passed the Durbar Arena by the time the Durbar would start. The Durbar was a festival of horsemanship in honor of the Emir, the spiritual leader of Igara. It was the time his subjects showed their loyalty and allegiance.

Early in the morning there were hardly any vehicles on the road. Alhaji knew he had to be very careful of the lone vehicle speeding down the road at that time of the morning. The drivers knew that Igara, being on a cattle route, there was every likelihood that they would come across cattle on the road. This did not stop them from speeding, often causing a fatal accident or most times, killing or maiming one or more of the cattle. Sometimes the cattle pusher or the driver was killed and the car a complete wreck. The day had started to break. Alhaji knew the palace guards would have started to arrive at the Arena with the local government officials to start arrangements for the day's festivities. He thought of how his household would have been up by now had he been at his Kafanchan home. They would have started preparing, as he would be one of the honored guests at Igara. By mid-morning he would have sent two heads of the cattle to the Emir as a gift for a successful Durbar Festival and as respect for being the ruler of Igara.

The day seemed to be moving fast. The cattle had not yet got into their paces; Alhaji had his hands full trying to get them into line. The herd was also trying to get used to following the leading cattle. Whichever one got out of line or wandered away Alhaji would quickly put him back with the others using his stick. Alhaji looked up at the sky. The sun had now come out to show that it would be a lovely day and a hot one at that. Alhaji Tijani continued to make haste slowly, stopping only by the well-known water hole at Igara to allow the herd to drink water to their fill. They had a long journey to go before the next water hole. By noon they had covered quite a distance and people had started to pass them on the road. At first it was one or two people then it increased to a few dozen people. The signs that the Durbar was taking place had started to show as the traffic to the arena had increased. Some were rushing in order to get a good sitting or standing position. Taxis were ferrying people to the ground; some luxury cars had also started to pass. Everyone seemed to be heading to the Durbar.

It was becoming obvious that the Durbar was almost ready. It was about to start. People were streaming into the grounds. The dignitaries and guests were arriving in their posh chauffeur driven cars. Some guests from abroad and some high government officials were in the VIP stands. They were already seated. There was an orderly confusion about the place. It was confusion to an untrained eye as to what to expect. It was a mass collection of colors. Drummers were drumming and entertaining the guests. The Horsemen were testing their horses. Some of their horses showed signs of restlessness. Everybody was turned out in their best clothes. Different colorful costumes added character to the occasion. Some horsemen with their decorated horses charged up and down the Arena. Trumpeters were blowing on their trumpets from different parts of the wide-open space. Each leading the different groups of invited men to the Durbar. A cacophony of noise was everywhere. A wooden white painted fence ringed the Arena.

The Emir started his grand entrance accompanied by his chiefs and his entourage of supporters. The palace staff, his drummers, trumpeters and other dignitaries made up the rest of entourage. The twirling large umbrella was held high above his head to protect him from the sun. The drummers drummed and the trumpeters blew to announce his royal presence and arrival. His subjects shouted praises and royal names at him as he made his way to his seat in the VIP lounge. All the guests stood as one. The Emir greeted them. Some guests came forward to pay their own special homage. It was a day his subjects paid him homage and rejoiced with him.

Far into the distance, barely seen but for a small cloud of dust, Alhaji Tijani was driving his cattle on the first leg of his journey to Lagos. He had glanced at the Arena and knew the Durbar was about to start. He could faintly hear the drumming and the trumpeting. He knew that if the Emir had been aware he was in town, the Emir would have insisted that he be present at the Durbar. He would have been one of the distinguished guests. Instead he had embarked on this foolhardily venture as his wife Fati had called it. Alhaji knew the beginning of the cattle push was the most important part. It was the time to settle the cattle down. It was the time to make them understand and obey his commands. It was also the time to understand the herd and to pray for Allah's guidance on the journey.

Alhaji Tijani had tried not to show any emotion to his family when he was leaving. Now his thoughts went again to his wife, his daughters Aminatu, Hauwa and his sons. He worried about them. He went over in his mind the arrangements he had made for them. He was satisfied. He also knew his son Ibrahim was capable and could take care of the family in his absence. Fati too was an industrious woman and could keep the family together. He snapped out of his thoughts.

"Hey, Jana hey!"

He shouted the signal to the lead cattle to keep moving. Alhaji had chosen the hardest way to push cattle, the almost impossible task of the lone pusher with the herd. In his days as a young pusher, he had done it alone a few times. He was respected for his skill and endurance on the trail. He enjoyed the adoration of the young pushers. It was on one of his cattle push that he met Fati and he never got tired of telling his sons of his exploits. Fati was a young Fulani maiden when he met her in her village. When he had made some money he had come back for her. He had known plenty of people on the route. Those were amongst the happiest periods of his life. He felt he had lived a good life and had worked hard. What he wanted now was to end his working life in grand style and enjoy the euphoria of having achieved a successful cattle push once more. There was no feeling like it, the feeling of success at the end of the journey. The Durbar was oblivious to Alhaji Tijani and his journey. The Horsemen charged at the VIP stand. They stopped a few feet away from the Emir, pulling up their horses. The riders paid homage to him while at the same time demonstrating their skill as horsemen. Wave upon wave of horsemen charged after one another to entertain the crowd. The crowd shouted and clapped for the riders while the Emir raised his fist in acknowledgement.

CHAPTER SEVEN

Clint woke up. It was 5:30am. He had had a rough night. Clint threw the cardboard sheet away. He had used it to cover himself and supplement with his blanket in the night. It had been a cold night. He sat up. He had slept by the side of a shop near the road. Clint remembered how he had arrived at Kafanchan in the night, walked around until he found a small restaurant to eat and then found a place to sleep for the few hours of the night that was left. Clint checked his gun and his bag. He adjusted his hat and looked around his surroundings. He spotted a public water tap and strolled over there. The children were already queuing to tap water for their parents. They watched him as he came and stood in the queue with them. They all looked at each other, looked at Clint and kept quiet. When it got to Clint's turn he rinsed his mouth, washed his face, then filled some water into his hat and turned it over his head. Clint was putting up a cowboy act for the children. He asked the last boy in the queue, who appeared to be the oldest, for the way to the cattle market. The boy described it to Clint and explained that he would have to walk since the buses had not started running yet. Clint turned and walked off towards the cattle market while the children started to giggle and laugh amongst themselves.

Clint walked for what seemed like ages. At first it had been dark with the house lights coming on one by one. Then the day started to break with people slowly coming out of their houses to go about their daily routine and to work. Day light broke and the morning sunlight came out. Clint noticed more and more people on the road with buses and trucks passing by. Since he had walked such a long distance he decided to leave the buses and complete the journey on foot. Some people stared at Clint; some made way for him, not quite knowing what to make of this oddity. Others pretended or did not notice him as they went about their business. After some time Clint stopped at a buka restaurant made of bamboo to eat. He ordered custard made from corn called pap and some fried plantain banana. When he had had his fill he moved on with his walk to the cattle market.

The sun was hot by the time Clint arrived at the cattle market where the cattle dealers met. Here, pushers were recruited to push cattle to different parts of the country. The whole place was empty but for a few people scattered around the market area. Clint walked over to where four cowhands were relaxing playing cards. They hardly paid any attention to him.

"Malam excuse me, I am looking for any of the cattle pushers."

The cowhands stopped their game. They looked Clint up and down. The look in their eyes was more of curiosity than of fear. The first cowhand nearest to Clint answered while continuing to play his game.

"There will be no market today; everybody has gone to the Durbar."

"Don't forget Alhaji Tijani," answered the second cowhand. "He was the only pusher that left."

"He left yesterday," answered the first.

The cowhands started to laugh. Clint could not understand why they were laughing.

"When I went to Igara yesterday, I passed him on the way. He was already grazing." They started to laugh again.

"Would he have gone far?" asked Clint.

"No, my guess is that he slept at Igara, to leave today," said the first cowhand

"That old fool can't make the journey alone," replied the second.

They both started to laugh again. Clint was puzzled at their amusement. He watched them for some time laughing and playing their cards. He didn't know what to say or the cause of their laughter.

The first cowhand continued,

"If you want to catch him, follow the crowd to the Durbar. On the other side of the arena, take a bus to Arewa. You will pass him on the way."

They stopped playing and looked at Clint who had made no move to leave them alone. The second cowhand whose turn it was to play advised Clint.

"You better hurry if you want to see him again."

Clint thanked them and walked away. They watched him pass the fenced gate. Clint walked towards the crowd heading for the Durbar. The cowhands looked at each other and shook their head in disbelief.

"Who was that stranger?" asked the first cowhand.

"Play your card or pay your money," replied the second cowhand.

They had been discussing Alhaji Tijani and his journey before Clint arrived. They knew Alhaji as a successful businessman and cattle dealer but did not know he had started on his road to success as a cattle pusher. They only found out when Alhaji arrived and started to select the cattle he needed for the drive. After watching the drama between Alhaji and his family, they saw him as a stubborn old man who was likely to get himself killed on the route.

A Cattle push on foot was a tough job. He was going to travel on foot from one part of the country to another. The journey was likely to last over a month. A month of grazing the cattle, sleeping out in the open, chasing strays from the herd, fighting with farmers, sometimes going without food and battling with the different illnesses that may afflict the pusher on the cattle drive. This was no job for an old man. Times had changed.

It would have been easier for Alhaji to use one of his trailers to transport his cattle. They wondered why anyone with money and of an advanced age would want to put himself through such unnecessary suffering. When Clint had gone, they talked about him also. They laughed at his clothes. They argued about his guns. Was it real? They wondered. They joked that the Durbar must have affected Clint in some way. Then they continued their game.

Clint had almost become desperate. He had to catch the cattle pusher before he entered the cattle path. If he happened to miss him, he would encounter a lot of difficulties in Kafanchan. Last night had been rough. In order to conserve his money he had eaten akara beans balls with bread. He had slept on the floor by a shop alley. He did not have a good sleep. He woke at the sound of the slightest noise. In fact he took a lot of risk in embarking on this journey he thought. Clint berated himself for not asking a little about the place before embarking on the journey. What more could he do? He wondered. He made his way to Igara. He did not know Igara was so far. He started to run. Although the Durbar had started the people were still streaming towards the arena. He meandered his way through the crowd. Those who saw him made way for him. His clothes made him stand out in the crowd. It was quite a distance from the Igara town to the Durbar arena. He urged himself on. He kept running. He felt he was losing time.

The sun had come out fully. He could hear the cheering and the clapping in the distance and knew he was near the Arena. His cowboy boots made it difficult for him to run faster. Once or twice he had keeled over on his heels. The excitement of the Durbar seemed to have gotten a hold on him. It helped him to quicken his pace. It was when he entered the gate that it occurred to him that he had never been to a Durbar. He had not given it a thought from the market place. There was no Durbar in Igandu. The crowd and the mass of colors were overwhelming. Using the VIP side he headed towards the opposite gate for the bus stop. A European woman sitting in the VIP area caught sight of Clint running through the crowd. Her eyes followed him as he weaved and bobbed, avoiding the palace guards and the police who were on duty. She was taken back, surprised at his clothes.

"Look over there. That's an African cowboy," she shouted to her husband while pointing to Clint.

They both watched Clint, speechless as he ran past the VIP stand. Only a few other people noticed the phenomenon. The others glued their eyes to the center of the arena where the different Chiefs of the Emirate were riding past with their entourage to pay their respect to the Emir. Clint continued to make his way out of the Arena towards where he thought the bus stop would be. It took him sometime to locate the bus stop. He had already lost half a day. He was impatient. Clint paced up and down. Some people passed him on the way to the Durbar. They must have thought his clothes were part of the dressing for the celebration of the Durbar. Clint wished for the bus to come. He did not want to go back to Kafanchan and wait again for another pusher the next day. His hopes had been raised. He had made the move and he had to follow it through.

CHAPTER EIGHT

The bus stop was completely empty except for Clint. He wondered if the bus would ever come, as he was the only intending passenger. The sun had started to go down. Clint had started to feel depressed. He had almost given up hope when he saw a bus coming; he resisted the urge to run towards the bus. The rickety old bus moving ever so slowly came and stopped beside him. Practically all the people in the bus alighted and headed towards the Durbar. Clint jumped into the bus and paid his fare. He went to sit at the front of the bus. He was not sure where he was going but he wanted to keep a look out for a Dan Fulani and his herd of cattle. The bus moved too slowly for his liking. Clint was getting impatient. He continued to search for the Dan Fulani. The man must be moving fast, he thought. After a long ride he finally sighted the pusher. He shouted for the bus to stop but the driver continued for almost another hundred yards. Clint jumped down and ran across to the path. He wanted to cut off the herd and meet the pusher head on.

The herd was moving over a grassy land in a leisurely pace. Alhaji kept pace with them. He watched them with keen eyes. He was beginning to feel young again. His mind was still on his family, though he battled within himself not to think about them. Then he saw Clint. At first Alhaji was not sure. In the distance was a man dressed in funny clothes standing with legs apart and with what looked like a bag over his shoulders.

"What am I seeing here?" Alhaji was talking to himself. "I must be getting old. I better be careful here."

Clint was straining his neck to see well. In an instant he could not see the Dan Fulani anymore. He started to walk down towards the cattle, slowly at first then picking up his pace, as he became anxious. He glanced to the left and then to the right but he still could not find the cattle pusher.

"He must be here somewhere," Clint said to himself.

This was the nearest Clint had ever got to a herd of cattle in his life. He cautioned himself to be careful. He decided that since he had made up his mind to come on this journey, to live the life of a true cowboy, then this was his first test. He had to go through with it. He felt since the cattle were not scared of him there was no need for him to be scared of them. Clint did not know that cattle could be so big close up. He closed his eyes.

The cattle continued to pass by his side. Alhaji made his way to the side of the herd and looked up. There again was the man he had seen standing in the middle of the road with the funny clothes. Alhaji bent down and quickly made his way into the middle of the herd. He used the big cows as his cover. He was peeking at Clint. Clint opened his eyes. The cows had almost passed him by. He felt since nothing had happened to him now, he was going to be alright. He walked to the end of the herd. The pusher was not there. Clint ran back by the side to the front. The pusher was not there either. Alhaji bent lower and ran towards the front of the herd. He was making his way through the cattle when they suddenly stopped. He was surprised and wondered why they had stopped.

He whispered slowly, "Hey Jana hey!"

The cattle still did not move. He shouted louder and they started to move. It was then that Clint saw him. The pusher was bent over, moving with the cattle and using the cattle as a shield. Clint smiled to himself. His cowboy outfit must have put some fear into the pusher he thought.

Alhaji continued to make his way to the front of the herd. Clint was smiling as Alhaji suddenly found himself looking at a pair of boots right in front of his eyes. He looked up until his eyes were fixed on Clint's gun, then he continued to Clint's eyes. Clint had put on his meanest cowboy look. The "Ron Cameron" look. Alhaji shouted so loud that the herd stampeded. They jumped all over the field running helter skelter until they collected themselves and chased their leader. Alhaji ran in the opposite direction heading towards Kafanchan. Clint ran in the other direction to Alhaji with the cattle giving chase behind him. His eyes were searching for a tree. He remembered so many times in cowboy films, a low tree branch had saved the hero from a stampeding herd of cattle. Clint could not immediately see one but headed for the nearest tree anyway. The stampeding cattle continued to chase after him. It must have been the biggest leap of his life as he held on to a fairly high branch. The herd passed the tree and ran far into the distance before Clint felt it was safe to come down. He could not imagine how he had climbed up the tree with his boots. Clint climbed down from the tree and decided to look for the Dan Fulani. The whole terrain looked deserted. He walked around for a long distance, searching.

He walked back all the way to the Durbar. The Durbar had finished and the Arena was deserted. Clint must have walked for a good two hours looking for the Dan Fulani. He walked over to the VIP stand and sat down. He had to rest a little. He wondered what to do with himself now. He blamed himself for the stampede, for still playing cowboys. He should not have put on his meanest look. It always frightened people. Now he had made the cattle to scatter. It would take the old man time to round up the cattle. His first attempt at joining a Fulani cattle push appeared to be ending in disaster. He adjusted his hat. He felt tired. Should he go back to Igandu? He wondered. He thought of the stampede again. He remembered the Dan Fulani was an old man. The sight of him running so fast and jumping up and down had to be seen to be believed. Clint cheered up a little. The stampede was real like in "Rawhide." He decided he would not give up. This was what he had come for. He would go and find something to eat. After the food, he would return to the Arena. He would sleep here tonight. The Dan Fulani could not have gone far. By the time he rounded up his scattered cattle he would have to rest and sleep. It would be too late for him to push on. Clint felt he would catch up with the pusher in the morning.

Clint dusted his clothes down with his hat and headed towards Igara. He felt good. He had had his first experience with cattle. He put the swagger back to his walk. He hoped the Dan Fulani would not be too annoyed with him when they finally meet up the next day. Clint hoped he would still be able to join the old man.

CHAPTER NINE

Clint woke up very early. He wanted to make an early start. He was sure that the pusher would leave early as pushers and their cattle traveled only in the day. He walked over to the trough that was kept for the horses to drink water. Clint at first poured some water on his face, then scooping the water with his hat, he poured it over his head. He adjusted his hat and set out for the bus stop. He did not have to wait long. It seemed the buses were running normally once again. He took the bus and came down where he thought the herd would be. He could not see them. Clint walked for quite a distance. He still could not see the herd. It amazed him that he had covered all this distance the day before while he was looking for the Dan Fulani. His eyes were going over recognizable signs on the terrain. The signs he could remember. In shock he realized he had been stepping on cow dung for some distance. Clint swore to himself and stopped to wipe his shoes on a stone.

He looked up into the distance and he saw the herd and the Dan Fulani. Alhaji had not slept well. He too had climbed up a tree when he saw the funny looking man coming his way after the cattle had stampeded. He watched the man pass the tree and concluded that the way the man was looking left and right he could have been out to kill him. When Clint had gone far towards the road to the Durbar arena, Alhaji had climbed down the tree and quietly but quickly rounded up his cattle. He went as far as was possible for him to go with the herd before nightfall and then he decided to find a suitable place to sleep. He ate a very light dinner and turned in early in order to be able to rise with the early birds. Throughout the night, he did not sleep very well. He kept waking up at the slightest noise. He had slept with his sword, dagger and poisoned arrow beside him. Even then, he was not sure that the man would not come back to try to kill him. It was a relief for him to see the morning light. He got up and started to prepare for his next stretch of the journey. By that stampede, the herd had slowed him down considerably. Many unexpected things were bound to happen on such a journey. In his early years as a pusher, he always expected the unexpected. He never expected that this would happen so soon after the start of his journey. The thought of Clint made him to instinctively look back. To his surprise, the man was there. The man appeared to be doing a form of ballet dance.

Clint had walked into a thick area of cow dung and was trying to pick his footsteps through the dung. Alhaji watched him for some time before he understood what Clint was doing. Alhaji started to laugh. It was the first time he had laughed since he left on the journey. He turned and continued leading his cattle forward. This foolish man could not be a killer, he thought. Every now and then, Alhaji would look back and see that the man was still following him but had managed to come out of the dung area. Alhaji decided to have some fun with this stranger and make things difficult for him. After all, I am an old, experienced cattle pusher, Alhaji reasoned. He soon noticed that Clint was a young man. He was just a bit younger than his son Dauda. There was no reason to be afraid.

"Allah is surely with me," he said aloud to himself.

He touched his sword to make sure it was still there. His amulets from his early days were round his neck and on his arm. He reassured himself that nothing could happen to him. They had never let him down. He touched the amulets. The man who had prepared them had since died. The power was very potent. Thanks to Allah, he never threw them away. Now they were working again to protect him. Alhaji praised himself that despite all Fati's attempt to throw them away, he had stopped her. He kept them among his private possessions, which no one dared to touch in his house. He watched Clint for some time and decided he was not afraid and if he had to, he would kill the young man.

Alhaji led the herd into a more dusty area of the terrain, smug in his knowledge that the herd would soon start to raise the dust towards Clint. Unaware of this, Clint soon began to cough until he realized that the cattle had been raising dust and he had walked right into it. He removed his handkerchief from his back pocket and tied it across his face to protect his nose from the dust. Alhaji smiled when he saw that he had succeeded. Clint smiled too when he remembered that the cowboys also covered their faces with a handkerchief in cowboy films. Clint continued following him. The dust started to clear. Clint had decided that he would continue to follow the herd until he got another opportunity to talk to the pusher. They walked like that for a long distance. Alhaji was in the front and Clint was at the back. Sometimes their walking pattern would change. They would find that they were walking parallel to each other only separated by the herd. In spite of all Alhaji's attempt not to look at the young man, he found it was very difficult. He would glance at Clint from the side of his eyes and when he discovered that the young man was also looking at him, he would quickly look away. Sometimes when Alhaji drew back, he found out that Clint was now walking in front of the cattle. They continued to interchange until Alhaji found himself again in the front and the young man once again at the back. Clint was already getting used to walking with the cattle. He did not know that Alhaji had not finished with him yet. Alhaji changed direction once again and led the herd into a very stony patch of road. Clint found himself tripping over the stones. The high heels of his boots would not allow him to walk properly. He stopped to check his heel and discovered that one of them was weak. It made it very difficult for him to balance. He started to limp towards the herd. Alhaji looked back and laughed with satisfaction. He would teach this young man a small lesson. He knew this terrain very well and from his inquiries about the route, he had an idea what to expect on the way. They would soon have to cross a stream. After that, the young man should give up.

He looked back again and Clint was still doggedly following behind him. Alhaji led the cattle for a very long distance. So far, Clint had made no attempt to get close to Alhaji Tijani and tell him what he was after. Clint had been thinking of the best way to approach the Alhaji. The first time had been more or less a disaster. He had now been going over in his mind not only how to approach Alhaji Tijani but what to say to him. There were many things he had not given much thought to. He had taken it for granted that it would be easy to approach a Dan Fulani and just tell him what he wanted. But now it did not look so easy. He would have to approach him cautiously and with tact so that he did not lose this once in a lifetime opportunity to join a Fulani cattle pusher. He had to find some way to approach him without panicking him. Clint also wondered how he would explain what he wanted to achieve. He was sure the Dan Fulani, by the look of things, did not know about the life of a cowboy.

He looked up and the Dan Fulani was far again into the distance. Whatever Clint wanted to say or do, he had to do it soon and get it over with. Alhaji led the cattle across the stream. Clint had felt relieved to come out of the stony area. He followed the herd into the water only to discover that in the middle of the stream, the water reached his knees and had entered his boots. He continued walking to the other side where he removed his boots to empty it of water. Alhaji who had been monitoring Clint's attempt to cross the water was once again beside himself with laughter. Clint was sure the Dan Fulani was laughing at him but it would not deter him. He would show him that cowboys don't give up. He put on his boots and followed.

The herd had turned the bend and had gone out of his view. He prided himself that once again, he was on a trail. He was not easy to shake off. He would track the herd like Davy Crocket or the Red Indian Scouts. They always got their man.

CHAPTER TEN

By the time Clint reached the bend, he found the herd grazing. Alhaji was sitting and resting under a tree. Clint decided to approach him. Alhaji saw him coming and raised his sword to show he was ready to defend himself. Clint raised both hands. The sword shook menacingly. Clint felt this pusher would not hesitate to use it. He also wanted to show the pusher he was not a threat. Alhaji used his sword to point at the gun. Clint nodded. Using his left hand, he undid the string holding the gun by his thighs and with the same hand, undid the buckle of his belt. He had seen Marlon Brando do that in "One Eyed Jacks." The gun dropped. Alhaji signaled him to move backwards. Clint obeyed. He stepped backwards, enough to indicate that he could not reach the gun. Alhaji got up from his sitting position and with his legs pulled the gun nearer to himself. He picked up the gun and examined it. Clint decided to put him at ease.

"It's not loaded."

Alhaji did not reply. He was still examining the gun. Clint spoke again,

"It doesn't fire real bullets."

When Alhaji had satisfied himself, he looked up at Clint.

"Who are you?" he asked.

"I am Clint."

Alhaji did not understand. It sounded like click to him.

"Click, Click why do you follow me?" he asked.

"They told me at the market you were pushing cattle to Lagos. I wanted to join you."

"Who told you? Did my sons put you up to this?"

"I met some people playing cards. They told me. They said everybody else had gone to the Durbar."

Alhaji was still suspicious that it was a trick by his sons. He wanted to get to the bottom of the mystery. He raised his sword higher threatening to strike and Clint raised his hands even higher.

"If you wanted to push cattle to Lagos why didn't you go to Kano and find work? There are many cattle dealers there looking for people to take their cattle to Lagos."

"I have never been to Kano or pushed cattle before. They will not trust me," replied Clint.

He hoped his answers would be acceptable.

"This is your first time?" continued Alhaji.

"Yes," replied Clint.

"How can I trust you, and why do you dress like that?"

"I am a cowboy," answered Clint.

Alhaji did not understand what Clint meant.

"Oh, you are not Fulani?"

Clint was beginning to feel his hands aching.

Alhaji continued,

"And you say you want to join me and you have never pushed cattle before?"

Alhaji's mind flashed back to his first cattle push. He had approached a cattle dealer and begged for a chance to learn to push cattle. It had taken time but he was given a chance in the end. He knew that if it had not been so, he might not be where he was today. He had pushed cattle that first time without pay, although when they got to Lagos finally, they gave him commission on the cattle that were sold. There was also a dash from the owner.

"I won't pay you," continued Alhaji.

"I don't need any pay. I just want to prove I can push cattle to Lagos."

In Clint's reply, Alhaji saw a bit of himself as a youth. For the first time, he took a good look at Clint. He always felt he was a good judge of character. The young man looked genuinely interested and he was completely ignorant of the job. Alhaji was sure the young man did not know the hazards he would meet on the way but he looked eager to learn.

"It's a long way to Lagos and you know nothing about cattle. It takes years to master how to push cattle."

"I am ready to learn and do as you wish." Clint indicated that his arms were aching

"You can put your hands down," ordered Alhaji.

"Thank you," replied Clint.

"Well I don't know," Alhaji was hesitant.

Clint did not know what to do again. His eyes pleaded for him.

"Look, if you don't trust me, keep my gun. Give it back to me in Lagos. It is my proudest possession."

Alhaji had since made up his mind to take Clint along but he did not want him to know yet. Clint continued, trying to give him cause to accept him.

"I have a little money. When I get to Lagos, I will find my way."

Their attention caught two Fulani milk maidens who appeared around the corner singing and laughing. Clint looked at the girls. They were different from the girls in Igandu. These girls had decorated their faces with traditional make-up. They had a long line in the center of their forehead down past their nose and down to their chin. Their lips were colored black and their cheeks had slight dabs of black make up. The girls were very light in complexion with long hair. Their short blouse barely covered the lower half of their breast and the long wrapping cloth was wrapped tightly round their waist accentuating their figure down to their legs. They were beautiful girls by any standard but Clint hardly noticed that. He had more on his mind and was concentrating on Alhaji and the sword. Alhaji put down the sword. He picked up the gun and put it in his bag which lay on the floor. He sat down again leaning against the tree. He indicated to Clint to sit down as the milkmaids attempted to pass.

"Come over here," he shouted at the milk maidens.

"Bring us some milk."

The girls stopped their singing and walked over. They served Alhaji and Clint two small calabashes full of milk. The girls looked at Clint, whispered to themselves about his clothes and smiled at him. Clint dipped his hat at them and smiled back. He got that from Gary Cooper. Alhaji paid the girls. They got up and walked away giggling and smiling at Clint. Alhaji looked at Clint and looked at the girls.

"Those girls like you."

Clint adjusted his hat and lowered it over his eyes.

"A cowboy doesn't get involved with girls. He always travels light."

"Oh is that so?" asked Alhaji.

"You people must live a hard life. I met my wife Fati, this way. She was a milkmaid. I used to pass their village on my cattle push."

After they had rested for some time in silence, Alhaji spoke again. He had been giving some thought about his journey.

"Well, okay you can join me. I do need an extra hand. I thought I would be able to push the cattle alone to Lagos. I had done it before in my youth. But I was wrong. Pushing cattle is a hard job and I am getting old. You have to make yourself useful. I will stay in front and you will bring up the rear until you have mastered that, then we will change. I will teach you what to do as we go along. I will teach you how to understand the cattle, how to speak to them and how to know their route by reading the stars and watching the sun."

Alhaji smiled to himself. He remembered his youth and his first day as a pusher. While they rested he asked Clint a lot of questions about himself and encouraged Clint to ask questions also. Clint asked about the push as much as he could. Alhaji Tijani advised him on what to take with him next time he would want to go on a push. He gave Clint an idea of what a push was like. He tried to make Clint understand the journey would be tough and full of danger. He was impressed by Clint's eagerness to learn and decided to teach Clint as much as he could on the journey. From their discussion, he realized Clint had an ambition to push cattle to Lagos just as he had done as a young man too. He did not understand much about the life of a cowboy but he could see the influence that way of life had on Clint, just as he as a young man was influenced by the life of a Fulani cattle pusher.

Alhaji noticed that Clint was not much of a talker. He felt that was good since in a push there was not that much time for talking. He would take the next few days to get to know more about the young man although talking to him was not too easy. Still Alhaji Tijani remembered his sons and how sometimes he found it difficult not only to talk to them but to understand them. He grunted and thought of the youths of today. Clint looked at him expecting him to say something but Alhaji did not.

CHAPTER ELEVEN

Their partnership started awkwardly. They had not gone very far before Clint felt his legs aching. He found he was easily tired and always needed to rest periodically. At those times he rested, Alhaji continued moving with the cattle. Alhaji could not afford to rest in his attempt to keep up with his schedule. At the same time, he wanted Clint to get used to the pace he wanted to keep. This was how he had started and this was the way he had learnt. Alhaji felt that Clint had to toughen up to be able to make it to Lagos. He saw Clint still trying to act the tough cowboy but knew that Clint would get over it by the time they got to Lagos. He would need to do that or give up going on a push altogether. He felt that Clint would not want to give up. He could see the determination in his eyes. Alhaji did not know how to tell him that the first few days were the easiest. The minute they entered the proper cattle route it became harder. Sometimes Alhaji would look back to see Clint almost a hundred yards behind, still resting. Alhaji would smile to himself, shake his head and mutter about the youths of today. When Clint caught up they would talk for a little while, as conversation between them was still awkward. They did not really have much to talk about yet. They were still feeling each other out when they did talk. Alhaji would ask how Clint was and how he was managing. They continued like this for a few days until they had to finally stop for a whole day.

Clint was grateful for the rest although he did not want to let Alhaji know how tired he was. Alhaji left the herd and came to meet Clint at the back. He pointed to a spot under the Kola tree.

"We rest here for the day. We will have a day's rest to replenish our stock before we continue."

They walked over and sat down. They sat in silence for some time. Alhaji knew Clint must be hungry. He was sure the boy had not had a good meal since he left the town Igandu, where he said he came from. After the first day on the road, he had shared his dry meat and bread with Clint. He turned down all offers by Clint to pay for his food. He wanted Clint to get used to the mode of eating when on a cattle push since they often went for days living on fruits or small animals they'd kill on the way. Often they are able to get some small foodstuff from farms which they cook. And often times they may push for a long while without food as is the case now.

Alhaji had deliberately not allowed them to eat for a long time to test Clint's will power. They had sometimes gone on fruits alone. But Alhaji still had a small piece of meat left. He looked into his bag and brought out some hard dried meat. He offered some meat to Clint. Clint accepted it gratefully. Alhaji then offered Clint some water to drink from his goat skin water gourd which also hung over his shoulder. Again Clint accepted it gratefully. Clint thought of how good Alhaji was to share everything with him. The one he valued most was the water. Although Alhaji had given him water on the way, he had been rationing the water. Alhaji had explained the need to ration the water since they may not easily come across drinking water on their route. He had also explained that not all water on the route is drinkable. Some are even poisonous. They may travel sometimes without water to bath. Clint now understood how important water was in his life and how he had taken it for granted in Igandu. Clint felt that if he was to go on another cattle push he must be prepared for water. These few days had shown him how unprepared and how ignorant he was about a cattle push. He wasn't sure but he was beginning to suspect these Dan Fulanis lived a tougher life than cowboys.

The first few days on the road Clint had been so tired that he often forgot to act the tough cowboy. When they had stopped in the evening he had often just fallen asleep where he had sat down to rest. Alhaji had let him rest without waking him up. In the morning sometimes Alhaji Tijani would start without him and Clint would have to race and catch them up. But lately Clint had started getting himself back. He had started to remember why he was on the road. He had started to put a swagger in his walk. Sometimes he would smack the cattle on the rump and shout "Giddy up." This would make Alhaji to laugh. Alhaji too was getting used to Clint's antics as a cowboy.

After they had eaten, Alhaji took out his blanket and spread it on the ground. He stretched and lay down on the blanket. The cattle were grazing and slowly settling down. Darkness had started to creep in and the moon was out. Clint had been thinking about cattle rustlers each time they stopped to sleep. He knew about them from cowboy films. He had been worried and could not hold it back any longer.

"Do I take first watch?" asked Clint.

Alhaji could not understand the question. He was puzzled. He looked at Clint. Clint explained further.

"I keep watch in case of cattle rustlers. This place looks a bit too open, cow thieves may operate."

Alhaji bent his head and raised his eyebrows.

"Cattle thieves," repeated Clint.

"Oh, cattle thieves," repeated Alhaji.

Alhaji started to laugh. He continued to pronounce the word 'rust' in an attempt at pronouncing rustlers. Clint could not understand the reason for the laughter. He knew in cowboy films rustlers were always stealing cattle.

"Who will steal the cattle? To where?" Alhaji asked. He still continued laughing making jokes and making comments.

"How will he carry it? Perhaps he would cook and eat it here."

This made Alhaji laugh even louder. Clint decided not to say anything more about rustlers.

"I better take first watch," he added.

Of course Alhaji knew Clint was correct in his fear of cattle thieves but he had wanted to teach Clint where he knew the lesson would be better absorbed and useful. He knew they were in an area where there could not possibly be any cattle thieves. He had been looking out for signs along the route but saw nothing. He feared that by the time they got into the areas where thieves operate, Clint might have put his guards down due to inactivity. There were well known routes where thieves and wild animals raided cattle herds. Alhaji knew those routes and he had also done his research well before he embarked on this cattle push. Clint got up and went to find a good spot to sit with a wide view of the terrain and the herd. He leaned his back against a tree and lowered his hat to his eyes. He squinted his eyes to give that look he had seen Clint Eastwood use in "A few dollars more." By then Clint Eastwood had become his idol and the whole gang called him Clint. Alhaji opened his eyes. He looked around until he saw Clint. He knew Clint was all right. Alhaji muttered to himself once more.

"Rustlers!" He shook his head and closed his eyes again.

Clint sat perfectly still watching. He watched as the cows took their sleeping positions one by one. After a while Clint found himself dozing. Sometimes he would nod his head and wake up. Try as he might to stay awake he continued to find he was dozing. Clint got up walked around to clear his head and check his surroundings. He wondered why he hadn't thought of rustlers before, after all he must have watched countless films where a posse had to be set up to go after rustlers. Sometimes the hero went after the rustlers on his own. He tried to remember the last film he saw where cattle rustlers took part but the title escaped him. He put it all down to exhaustion and tiredness after all he knew his films. He knew the cowboy films and their titles. Clint walked to the base of a big mango tree and sat down underneath. He noticed the unripe mangoes were still small. He glanced over to where Alhaji Tijani was. Alhaji was already asleep. Clint covered himself with his blanket and pulled his hat down on his face. Before long, Clint dozed off again.

Alhaji heard the loud scream and woke up at once. He sat up immediately searching for Clint. He checked where he had last seen him. Clint was jumping up and down and shouting. He was beating his body with his hat and with his hands. Alhaji could guess at once what had happened. He ran over to Clint. He pushed Clint down to the ground and helped him remove his shirt. It took them time to remove the trousers because of the boots. When the boots came off Clint removed his trousers. He followed Alhaji's example and helped to shake down his clothes. Alhaji explained that ants must have bitten Clint. He knew Clint was in pain as he could see the swelling coming up on Clint's body. Alhaji took Clints blanket and shook it down. They collected the rest of his belongings and they walked back together to where Clint had sat. There they noticed a long line of soldier ants climbing up the mango tree. Alhaji explained that Clint must have sat on their marching route. He took Clint to where he had kept his bag. He took out a black liquid he kept in a bottle and rubbed the liquid over the swellings and bites on Clint's body. Then he brought out some dried roots and gave them to Clint.

"Chew this. It will soon stop the pain."

Clint took the stick and started to chew. He did not mind that it was bitter. Alhaji sat down on his blanket. He shifted to the side to make room for Clint.

"Sit down on the blanket. You will soon be fine. Never sit under a mango tree at night. It harbors a lot of insects. A lot of them bite."

Clint stored the information in his mind. He would not make that mistake again. Alhaji knew that Clint would find it difficult to sleep. He did not tell Clint that the roots would help him to sleep. He decided to keep Clint's mind off the pain by talking to him.

"Did you know that once on a night like this I was bitten by a snake?"

Clint looked at Alhaji surprised.

"My master Amidu had to suck the venom out. I learnt a lot about medicine and treatment from him. Apart from being a cattle pusher he was also a skilled herbalist. I have medicine for snake bites, insects, scorpions and many others in my bag. I will teach you those too but it will have to be slowly. It takes time to master them."

"How do you know when there is a wild animal around? Supposing you are asleep?" asked Clint.

"There are many signs. When the birds rise up together at once to the sky, it is a sign of danger. When the cattle gather together pushing the little calves to the middle, it is a sign also that a wild animal is coming." A cow mooed not too far away from where they sat. It attracted their attention but the herd was still.

"If cows continue to moo for some time it is a sign that they are thirsty. Always remember that."

Clint nodded. He was beginning to feel sleepy again. He fought against the feeling. He wanted to keep listening to Alhaji. Without thinking he leaned back on the blanket to get more comfortable.

"Do you ever have to kill a cow?" he asked.

"Cattles die for many reasons on a push. When they are lame, you may have to kill them. Sometime when there is no food, like if you are in the desert and you cannot go on after days without food, you are forced to kill one to eat. There are some areas near the border where soldiers from the other countries raid. They often steal cattle from the pushers forcefully. More especially if they are fighting a civil war in their country and their army needs food. A lot of cattle are lost that way. You don't have to worry about that though since we will not be going near any borders."

Alhaji looked at Clint. Clint had fallen fast asleep. His head was resting on the blanket. Alhaji shook his head and smiled. He lay back on the blanket and tried to get some sleep too. He had to awake up very early in the morning.

CHAPTER TWELVE

The sun had risen early. Clint felt something wet touch his ears and woke up. At first he thought he was dreaming. He found himself looking straight into two huge eyes. Clint screamed in fright and started to roll away from the monster. When he had stopped shouting and rolling, he discovered that the monster was a big bull that had touched his head. He looked around; Alhaji was nowhere to be found.

Alhaji had woken up, and had gone quite a distance with the herd. Clint quickly dressed, put on his shirt, his bag over his shoulder, and raced after them. He soon realized that the bull was still behind. He ran back, smacked the bull on its buttocks and both of them ran after the herd. Clint ran over to Alhaji at the front.

"Enjoy your sleep?" asked Alhaji

"Yeah, why didn't you wake me?" replied Clint.

"I didn't sleep most of the night. I must have fallen asleep when you were talking to me. You should have woken me."

"I sent Gala to wake you," said Alhaji.

Alhaji knew Clint had slept. He had slept deeply. It was good for him to have rested.

"The bull?" asked Clint.

"Yes. His name is Gala. How is your body now? The swellings have gone?"

"Yes I feel okay now," said Clint.

"Thank you. You must teach me about herbs and roots."

"Yes I will," said Alhaji.

They kept walking, maintaining the pattern they had been following and heading towards the River Niger. When they drew level again, Clint wanted to know more about cattle, the plants, the animals they might come across, the insects and anything Alhaji could teach him. He was never tired of learning.

"Why don't you teach me more about the herd?"

"What is there to teach? You are already learning as you go along. I have also been teaching you by allowing you to learn by yourself. You have to take it slowly."

"Give me some pointers to remember, I don't forget the pointers."

Alhaji smiled. He liked Clint. The young man wanted to learn.

"You see that cow in the front? That is called Jana. Jana is brown. Over there is Bokolo. Bokolo has no horns. Ambala has small horns and Kuyi has no hump. Can you remember all that?" asked Alhaji

"Yes please go on." Clint was enjoying the lesson.

"Muturu is short and Jali is a very wicked cow. When he is annoyed, he is ready to die. If you hold a red cloth in front of him, he will charge at you. Each cow has a name, always remember that."

"What about that cow over there?" asked Clint.

Now that he had got Alhaji talking, he did not want Alhaji to stop.

"That one is Gala."

Clint could guess the meaning of Gala, so he

quickly added.

"Gala means white."

"Yes you are correct," Alhaji laughed.

"Do they have a leader?" Clint asked.

"No, but whichever cow is the strongest gets the respect of the others. He becomes the leader. Each bull is nine times stronger than a man. Do you know a cow believes humans cannot kill it but only God can? Once you turn it down on the ground and turn its head it surrenders its life to God."

They both became quiet for some time. They were both thinking of that last statement, Alhaji more so than Clint. He had become more religious lately. The statement also touched Clint. He too felt more respect for the cows. He was not very religious but was learning a lot on this trip.

"They seem to respect the stick?" Clint said that as a form of question.

He had observed how Alhaji had used the stick to control the herd many times.

"Oh, the stick," replied Alhaji.

"Without the stick, you cannot control them. They are trained from birth to respect the stick. There are powerful cows that cannot be controlled by ordinary stick. You need a stick with its own power. The traditional priest or Alfa will give you the power."

Again they fell silent.

CHAPTER THIRTEEN

Pushing cattle with Alhaji Tijani was an education on its own. Clint was learning fast. He watched Alhaji closely. He listened to instructions and took corrections whenever he went wrong. They pushed the cattle during the day and slept at night. Clint's fear of the cattle soon disappeared completely. He started to understand them. He had picked up the language Alhaji used to move the cows or to give them instructions. At night he slept with the cattle using them as a shield against the cold night wind. When the cattle were grazing he would stand with them, watching them, protecting them and trying to get used to their names. He knew the stubborn ones and the quiet ones. Sometimes he would help them along and direct them to where the grass was better. Alhaji taught him how to read the moods of the cattle. More signs to look out for when there is danger. He taught Clint how certain birds in the sky can warn the cattle of danger.

They pushed the cattle through the different terrains of the North. Soon they found themselves in the desert. There were times Clint thought he would die of thirst and hunger. Alhaji seemed to know everything. Clint was amazed how Alhaji recollected things he had done many years ago. Alhaji showed him how to collect dew from plants to drink. Clint learnt how to manage water. For food they lived on rodents and reptiles. Days and weeks went by as they continued on their way to Lagos.

They passed Fulani settlements and villages with their cluster of mud huts and thatched roofs. Sometimes when people saw them, they would stop and stare at Clint. Alhaji would smile and shake his head. They pushed through the lush green savannahs of the North. Sometimes they walked together. They would talk and tell stories about each other, funny stories that made their journey less tedious. Alhaji would point out different landmarks. He taught Clint other different points he should know. He taught him about vegetation. They would walk together behind the herd. When it was time to rest, they would stop. The cattle too needed to rest and graze. Alhaji taught Clint how to set a fire and how to prepare what they would eat.

Some days they walked all day. Clint often wondered where Alhaji got all the energy and strength from. For a man of his age he was still very agile. Clint also noticed that Alhaji was being pushed by the will to succeed. A will not to disappoint himself. He did not want to disappoint the family. He did not want to be a failure. He wanted to prove to himself that he could push cattle to Lagos again on his own. He wondered how Clint could walk all these rough terrain and distance with his boots. Clint had been a good actor. He did not want Alhaji to know when his feet ached. Sometimes his feet would stiffen and he would find it difficult to walk. These were the times he preferred to make his way to the back of the herd where Alhaji would not see him. But Alhaji saw everything. He did not want to embarrass Clint. When Clint was not keeping pace, Alhaji would slow down to help him. At times he would stop the herd altogether. All in all, Alhaji felt Clint was coming along just fine as a pusher. He had started to get fond of the cattle. He had also overcome his fear of wild animals attacking the herd at night. Clint had been overly protective to the cattle. Clint loved it when Alhaji told him stories of some legendary pushers.

Alhaji too was enjoying himself. He was now well into his stride. They were making good time and keeping to the schedule he had worked out. They were covering a lot of ground and putting hundreds of kilometers behind them. Alhaji was more than convinced now that they would both make it to Lagos. This was the first time Clint had left his state to see other parts of the big country and he loved every bit of it. Sometimes he thought of his pals in the Cowboys and wished they were with him to experience what he was experiencing. Once or twice they passed farms where the farmers had given them foodstuffs. In one or two settlements the spiritual leader, the Alfa or Imam had said prayers for them to wish them good luck. Clint was impressed that Alhaji Tijani was very spiritual and rigorously kept to his prayer times except when the situation forced him to miss it. At the times Alhaji did his ablutions, Clint would move away to give him privacy. Clint had tried to rationalize why he hadn't been religious but reasoned it was not his fault. He had not been brought up with religion and none of the Cowboys had been religious.

At some towns, Alhaji Tijani would leave Clint with the herd grazing while he went to town or to the market to get whatever they may need on the way. Sometimes when there was time, he left Clint to go to the mosque. They passed big towns, small towns, crowded and densely populated towns. Some others were sparsely populated.

Each was a wonder on its own to Clint, each was a discovery. Sometimes they had to go far from the towns to get to grazing land. Other times they would be forced to graze the cattle by the tarred roadside risking one of the cattle from being knocked down by a speeding vehicle. Other times it would be a long trek to get to water for the herd and for Alhaji and Clint. The weeks rolled by and the vegetation and the climate changed too. It changed from the savannah to the dense forest, from the rainy season to the hamattan and dry season. They passed other pushers on the way. The pushers would tell them what the roads were like and what to look out for. Sometimes they would share food with them. There was a kind of family and camaraderie amongst the cattle pushers. Clint felt like one of them. Alhaji would explain about Clint to them and he would try the best he could to explain that Clint was a cowboy. After the explanation they would give Clint more respect and share their food with him. They would accept him as a brother. Clint was amazed at the long stretches of tarred road in some states seemingly leading to nowhere or to the horizon. At those times it was as if the trek would never stop. Some areas were so desolate and lonely that when a bird flew past it was an event. One was happy to see some movement. The thing Clint feared most was the speeding luxury passenger buses. With their passengers they sped past to the next town or state. They passed with such speed that the force of the displaced air hit you, forcing you off your stride. This was when he feared most for the cattle.

Once in a while on the route, Alhaji Tijani would make a quick detour to ask about someone he remembered from his youth. Clint learnt so much. He learnt about the stars. They used the stars to find their way. The journey had also made Clint to be aware of the smells of the environments. Different terrains had different smells and so too the towns and villages. He learnt how to eat roasted bugs and raw vegetation. He ate fruits he had never seen before. And best of all he learnt how to treat cattle when they fell sick. Clint felt he was becoming a true cowboy but that his lesson would be complete when they entered Lagos with the cattle.

CHAPTER FOURTEEN

The breeze had become cooler. Alhaji told Clint it was a sign they were nearing the river. By their left, in the distance, hidden by a clump of trees was a village.

The tops of the thatched roofs could be seen just above the high bushes of the forest. Clint could hear a lot of drumming and faint shouting in the distance.

"What could be happening at that village?" he asked, turning to Alhaji.

"There must be some form of celebration going on. If I remember the village well, then we should sight the river any time now."

They walked only a short distance before the shining water reflecting from the sun came into their view. The sun coming through the trees gave out a beautiful picturesque image, throwing shadows on the ground. They walked downhill on the footpath between the trees and the bushes towards the river. When they broke through into a clearing on level ground, Clint now took a good look at the river. Although the sun shone on the river and the rays reflected into his face Clint could see the water was grey in color. He judged by a tree branch he could see floating in the water that the river was flowing from right to left. Clint was overawed by the size and sheer force of the river. He had not seen water so vast and stretching in to the distance in his life. From where the bushes and the grass ended the ground became sandy leading on to the water's edge. In the middle of the river there appeared to be two sandy islands. A few mud huts were scattered on the islands. Alhaji saw Clint staring at them in surprise and explained that the canoes belonged to the fishermen that fish on the river. They built the huts during the dry season, which we have now and use them during breaks in fishing to rest. Because of the dry season, the level of the water goes down. This is what has caused the two islands to emerge. During the rainy season the water level goes up and the islands are submerged. Alhaji explained that during his youth, the islands were not there but because of the dam that was built further up to hold the water and generate electricity, there is now less water coming down. He explained to Clint that the Government wanted to dredge the river to make it deeper so that big boats could travel down to the towns by the river.

"We will still meet this river at Okuta where we are going to catch the trailer."

From Okuta, the water goes to the tributaries where it separates and makes its way to the ocean. The ocean is very mighty." Alhaji explained.

Clint was excited. He knew this would give him a chance to have a bath in the river. He hadn't had a good bath for a few days.

"Is the water deep?" he asked.

"I need a bath."

"That's the River Niger. We are all going to have a bath. It's less deep to your left."

Alhaji found his knowledge of a push was still very much with him. After so many years and facing his business, his memory was still very good. He was glad he undertook this journey and he was enjoying Clint's company. Clint was always excited and full of questions.

"Can the cattle swim?" he asked.

Alhaji nodded. "They can swim better than you and me. If you enter the water and call them, they will follow."

"What if they don't want to swim?"

"If they are swimming and one turns back, know that they have no more strength to swim further. You don't force them."

Clint raced away, taking off his boots and clothes as he was running. The water looked inviting. Feeling uninhibited, he jumped naked into the river. To his surprise, the herd soon entered the water. He looked around for Alhaji. Alhaji came beside Clint to show him he was a very good swimmer. While Clint was bathing, Alhaji directed the cattle to cross the river at a very shallow end. Clint climbed out of the water and went back to collect his clothes. He started to dress. Alhaji led the herd across the part of the river that had dried up. Clint kept his eyes on them. As he was about to follow, he thought he heard voices.

He stopped what he was doing and listened carefully. He did hear voices. He made his way towards the direction of the voices. There were about ten hefty men there and an old man who appeared to be pouring libation on the ground. There was another group of men carrying musical instruments and standing away from them. One of the ten men was holding a chicken in each hand. They appeared to be standing in front of a shrine. The blood from the chicken was pouring on the floor of the shrine. Clint moved as close as he could without being seen. For the moment, he had forgotten Alhaji and the herd. An old man was speaking in front of the shrine. From what Clint could understand, he was praying to the gods and their great ancestors who were wrestlers to accept the libation so that the day would be victorious for their village. The musicians started to play. Only one of the hefty men was dancing. Everybody fell in behind him as he led the group out of the shrine heading for the village. Clint decided to follow them for a little while. He was curious to know what was going to happen. He would catch up with Alhaji later. Alhaji and the herd had gone into the distance.

Clint followed the group discretely. When they arrived at the village, he noticed there was a wrestling festival going on. There were different musical groups leading their own village champions. The whole village was full of gaiety. The younger wrestlers were just ending their bouts. The people were clapping. As the group he had followed entered the village square, the whole place exploded with more shouts and clapping. Clint reasoned the hefty man at the front must be the favorite. Clint removed his boots and hung them over his shoulder by the straps. Then he climbed a tree to have a good view without being noticed.

The two main wrestlers were soon locked

in battle. The music raised the atmosphere to frenzy. The wrestlers did not give each other any quarter. They demonstrated their skills. The women seemed to be enjoying the contest the most. Finally, the tension eased when the wrestler Clint saw by the river won. The whole village was thrown into commotion as people left their seats to go and carry him shoulder high.

It was then Clint remembered the herd. He climbed down quickly, put his boots back on and ran back towards the river. He crossed at the shallow and dry area where he had seen Alhaji drive the cattle through. He soon picked up the trail of the cattle, running without stopping until he had caught up with them. Clint was panting and smiling. He could not wait to tell Alhaji what he had seen. But he had missed the most exciting part of the wrestling contest when a beautiful young maiden was presented to the winning wrestler as his prize and his Bride.

CHAPTER FIFTEEN

"Where have you been?" asked Alhaji.

"I saw some wrestlers and followed them to the village. I watched a very exciting wrestling contest," answered Clint.

"In the old days you could see many wonderful things on a cattle push. There was no experience like it. You are lucky. You are experiencing something that is dying out in the country. Now cattle herds go by trailer. You put your cattle on a trailer and whoosh in a few hours you are there. Enjoy this push my son. Enjoy the freedom, enjoy the air, and enjoy the stars, the land and its people. The real achievement is at the end of the journey. You will be one of the last of a dying breed. How would you say it? The last of the cowboys."

Alhaji laughed at his joke. Clint was moved again. Alhaji really loved the life of a Dan Fulani.

"Alhaji, you too, you are a cowboy."

Alhaji laughed even louder. But Clint meant it. He saw Alhaji as the cowboy. He was glad he came on this trip. Clint's relationship with Alhaji had been getting stronger and stronger. It was becoming a father and son relationship. Clint was beginning to care for the old man too. This was the first time he really cared for anybody. It was different from how he felt for the gang. Alhaji too had been feeling closer to Clint. He used to look at Clint. He had been studying him. He felt Clint was lonely. He had not talked about himself much and Alhaji wanted him to talk on his own volition. He talked a lot about the cowboys but not really about himself, his family or his people. They had walked almost an hour before Clint broke the silence.

"I saw a film once. The Last of the Mohicans."

"Were they cowboys too?" asked Alhaji.

"Yes Alhaji and they were Red Indians.

They both laughed again.

"What are Red Indians?" asked Alhaji.

Clint had wanted to explain but there was a way Alhaji was laughing that attracted Clint's attention. He did not look his old self. Clint wondered why he had not noticed it before.

"Alhaji what is wrong? You don't look too good."

"Oh nothing much," replied Alhaji.

"I just feel a little cold."

Clint looked up at the sun and then looked at Alhaji. Alhaji was sweating. He wondered why Alhaji should be cold.

"Well, you don't look too good to me."

"I am fine. We will soon reach where we can rest."

Clint took his word for it and drew back to bring up the rear of the herd. One of the cattle had strayed. When he rounded up the cow, he could not see Alhaji in front. He searched around the herd and noticed him sprawled on the ground. The cattle had stopped moving. Clint raced over to him and made him sit upright.

"Alhaji, are you alright?"

"I think I have fever, I have felt it coming for some time."

"Then we must rest."

Clint helped Alhaji get up and walk to the shade. Using the bags, he tried to make Alhaji comfortable. Clint was confused and afraid. He did not know what he would do if Alhaji could not continue. Alhaji pointed to the bush.

"Go over there to the pawpaw tree. Bring some of its leaves. Then collect some of the lemon grass. Bring a pot full. We will cook them."

Alhaji untied a small bowl from his bag and put it down.

"What does it do?"

"I will drink it and it will control the fever till morning."

Clint ran into the bush and started to gather pawpaw leaves. After that he gathered the lemon grass and some wood. Then he collected the bowl and went to search for water. It took some time before he could find a stream. He took the water back in the bowl. Following Alhaji's direction, he put the leaves and the grass in the bowl.

Taking a matchstick from Alhaji's bag, he struck it against his boot, cowboy style. He had seen it done so many times before. Alhaji checked that the fire was burning well then he turned to Clint.

"Go over and see that the herd is okay. Take my stick."

Clint hesitated; he knew what the stick meant to Alhaji.

"Go on and take it." Alhaji made to stand up.

Clint took the stick to keep Alhaji from standing up and went over to settle the cattle. After settling them, Clint went over to the fire. He took the bowl and proceeded to give Alhaji the drink. At first, it was too hot but he continued to coax Alhaji into drinking the pawpaw leaf and lemon grass brew. Alhaji was embarrassed at his situation.

He tried to give reasons as to why he was in this condition.

"I must be getting old. In my younger days, I would push this herd even with my eyes closed."

Clint gave him some encouragement. Their roles were reversed. Clint was in charge now.

"In the old days, it took over a month to cross from Maiduguri to Lagos".

Clint found a comfortable place to sit. Alhaji continued talking. Clint thought the fever was too high and Alhaji was becoming delirious. It was a new experience for him, to have to take care of somebody. He wasn't sure of what to do, but he did not want Alhaji to find out.

"This is my first push in over forty years. I am just a stubborn old fool. My family warned me not to take this trip but I wouldn't listen. My customers said I would die on the road."

"You will be alright Alhaji, we will make it."

"I am giving up the business. I want to hand it over to my sons when I get to Lagos. I only wanted to relive how I started. The cattle business has become monotonous to me. The old ways are changing. What is left for an old man like me? The cattle used to come from Sokoto, Chad, Niger, Maiduguri, Bauchi and Gongola. You would buy from different villages and herd them together."

Clint was silent. He did not know what to do but felt after a while the fever would come down. He hoped Alhaji would soon regain his old self.

"Clint, do you have a family?"

Clint was surprised at the question. Alhaji's eyes had been half closed and Clint thought he would have fallen asleep to let the medicine go to work.

"I don't have any family. My parents died when I was a child."

It was a lie Clint told everybody. But to him his parents were as good as dead. He did not know where they were and if he saw them on the road he would not recognize them. Since he ran away from his uncle he had never looked back. He had no wish to see them and did not miss them or his uncle.

The stick fell from Clint and he leaned over to pick it up.

"How did you get into the cowboy business?"

At first, Clint did not want to answer then he changed his mind and opened up.

"I was brought up by my uncle. We lived in Ibado, just over a day's journey from Igandu and it was a small village. He didn't treat me too well so I ran away. I ended up at Igandu where I met our leader Kimosabi."

"That's a funny name."

"Yes, it's his cowboy name. It means the master who knows all. I liked the way he walked and the way he talked. He had a group of boys who were always hanging around him. One day we decided to come together as a gang and to dress like cowboys. It was just for fancy, for a festival. From the day I went to the cinema and watched my first cowboy film, I knew that was the life for me. We swore allegiance to our group. The gang became my life we called ourselves "The Cowboys."

Alhaji was always philosophical. He counseled Clint.

"Once a cow is born, after its first day break, it is free to go anywhere. You have now experienced your first day break."

Clint was silent for some time. He wanted to think and assimilate what he had just been told. Alhaji prodded him to keep talking.

"Go on, tell me more."

"Well the gang in those days would walk around the town playing tough and putting fear into people. They feared us. They thought our guns were real. Once we discovered that this was the case, we decided to make use of it. If we could get work from it, we could always feed ourselves. We then became a security force for hire. We provided guard duty on big occasions and in the cinema houses. This got us into the cinema free. We would go anywhere we wanted. It stopped us from stealing."

Clint looked up and Alhaji was fast asleep. He covered him with the blanket and stoked the fire. He sat down, lowered his hat and watched Alhaji breathing. It was heavy. He knew he would not get much sleep that night. Clint was sure Alhaji had not heard half of what he said. Throughout the night he kept the fire going, made sure Alhaji was well covered and wiped the sweat from his forehead regularly. Mosquitoes too did not let Clint sleep. He was kept company by the noise and the shadows of the night.

CHAPTER SIXTEEN

Alhaji was the first to wake up. He was still not feeling very well. He had slept fleetingly and was aware that Clint had been up almost all the night. The fever was still inside him. He knew it was serious. The pawpaw leaves had done him good but what he needed was at least a few days rest in bed with some good treatment. He was worried about having to leave Clint and the cattle and he had spent most of the night thinking about it. This had contributed to his lack of sleep. He had to have treatment otherwise he might not make it to Lagos. Clint could go on or wait for him. As soon as he was well he would join Clint and the herd.

"Click?"

Clint jumped up immediately, surprised to see Alhaji up. He was embarrassed that he had slept off.

"Click, I have to get to the nearest village for treatment. If I don't get it, I will not make it."

"How far is the village?"

"Not too far. I remember it vaguely."

Clint was worried. So many things were going through his mind. He was afraid but he dared not show it.

"You are sick Alhaji. I will come with you to the village."

"No. I will make it." Alhaji answered firmly to let Clint know his mind was made up.

Clint also knew Alhaji was stubborn and could not be made to change his mind easily.

Alhaji continued,

"You must take the cattle and head for the bridge at Okuta. Dauda my son will be there with the trailer. If I don't make it, they'll panic. You are my only hope. I will join you back on the way or at Okuta, but if you don't see me, tell them what happened."

"I don't know the way and I don't think I could push the cattle without you".

Alhaji looked Clint straight in the eye.

"You are a cattle pusher now. You can make it. I know you can. Listen very carefully, if you have problems, speak to the cattle. They are well trained. They will understand you. Talk to Gala, Gala is almost human. Do not worry for the cattle; they sense danger even before you do. I have taught and shown you a lot already. I know you can do it. Let me go over some points again with you."

Clint listened with rapt attention.

"They eat anywhere and can go up to three days without food. If the leading cow diverts from the track, the others believe bad luck is ahead. Follow the bush path in the day. At night mark the brightest star and where it is pointing. Use the three small stars nearest to it to understand the direction you should take. I have shown you how to do that. Always be up before the cattle. Don't allow them to get lazy."

Alhaji staggered a little, Clint rushed to his aid. Alhaji motioned that he was okay. He mustn't give Clint cause to worry. He knew Clint had a big job on his hands. It was a challenge but he was confident Clint could make it. He had seen those qualities in him after a few days of being together. Alhaji remembered an important point.

"At Atanu, you will come across a veterinary. Pay and have the cattle checked. Remind me to give you the papers for the cattle. I kept it somewhere. Make sure you collect your receipt. You will present it whenever it is required. Always use the marks on the cattle to identify them. That way you will not get confused. When you reach Oburu, look to your left, you will see a railway track. There will be water up front. If you are lost, ask for directions. You may meet other pushers on the way. If I don't meet you before then, I will be on the bridge waiting with Dauda for you. Here is some money. Good luck."

Clint took the money.

Alhaji embraced him and started to leave. Clint shouted after him.

"Good luck Alhaji."

Alhaji stopped, turned round and came back to Clint. He removed the amulet from his arm.

"Wear this amulet. It will help and guide you. And use the stick well. It has its own power and cows respect it. Now go."

In their anxiety for each other, they both had forgotten about the papers for the cattle.

CHAPTER SEVENTEEN

Alhaji turned and headed through the bush towards the village. Clint watched him go. Clint was in a daze. He turned and looked at the herd. He instinctively said,

"Hey Jana hey!"

The cattle started to move. His mind flashed to "Wagon Train." The wagon leader always shouted "Wagons Ho" and they started to move on the trail. He smiled to himself. Yes he was a cowboy now, a true cowboy. The task ahead of him was daunting but he will make it. "Clint Eastwood" always made it, the "Cisco Kid" made it and "Bronco Lane" made it, so there was no way he too would not make it.

"Hey Jana hey!"

Clint noticed that the heels of one of his boots had started to give way again. He finally decided to remove them. He tied the laces together and hung them over his shoulders. He pushed the cattle into the bush path and before long he could not find his way. It took Clint more than two hours trying to find his way out. He pushed to his left and then to his right and still there was no path. Then he remembered Gala.

"Gala, come on boy. Gala come on. Show the way Gala."

Gala came out of the herd and led the others to the correct path.

They went on their way, resting when necessary. At first, he was afraid to sleep alone. He stayed awake trying to make sure none of the cattle was stolen or lost and none wandered away. The days appeared to be longer and the push more tiring. Most of the time Clint tried to keep his mind occupied. This was the best time to go over his life and to think of the Cowboys. He remembered things that happened all the years he was with the Cowboys. Incidents that had formed a land mark in his life. Clint remembered some funny moments and some sad ones. He wondered what the Cowboys would be doing now. He thought of his friend Roy Rogers and hoped he would be alright. Clint wondered what it could have been like had the cowboys been on this trip with him. Could they have coped? He concluded they would after all. The Cowboys were a tough bunch. He thought of the individual members of the gang. The good times he had with them. Clint realized that now he actually missed them. Maybe it was the loneliness of pushing cattle without Alhaji.

He reprimanded himself for feeling sorry for his condition after all this was what he had wanted and he had got it. He was now experiencing the life of a Fulani cattle pusher. They were the nearest to the true Cowboys and here he was on the road living the life of a true Fulani cattle pusher. He was a real cowboy and it was all thanks to Alhaji Tijani. No matter how much his mind wandered or how much he wanted to keep his mind on the push his thoughts always wandered back to Alhaji and hoping he would be alright. At those times, Clint continued to go over in his mind what Alhaji had taught him. He used Alhaji's instructions. He thought about Alhaji a lot. He was like the father he had always wanted. He would not let Alhaji down. He was going to make it to the bridge.

They went through the thick forests. This had taken him a few days to clear. It was a in village near Barkulu town that Clint ran into his first major problem. The herd had entered a farm by mistake. Three farmers working on their farm had seen them and started to throw stones at the herd. One of the stones hit the lead bull. It jumped up and charged away. The others followed and they ended up in a stampede. Clint was left standing alone. It happened so fast. Before he could get himself together, a stone also hit him in the head and he was knocked unconscious. The farmers seeing Clint in his cowboy outfit and unconscious took to their heels. They had not seen a pusher like that before. Clint had remained unconscious for about an hour.

Dark clouds were moving fast across the sky. The breeze was getting stronger and it was threatening to rain. A few drops of rain had started to fall. They fell at an angle due to the force of the wind. Clint was still lying unconscious on the ground. The raindrops continued to hit his face like hailstorm. When Clint regained consciousness, it took him some moments to get his bearings. He looked around and discovered the herd was scattered all over the place. He shook his head to remove the slight feeling of dizziness.

Then he ran over and started to round up the cattle. The rain beat a staccato rhythm against the trees. The branches of the trees were bent over backwards as if they were about to snap from the force of the wind. Clint struggled against the wind as he rounded up the cattle. The dark rain cloud soon broke and a heavy downpour suddenly covered the terrain. Clint struggled in the rain, running from one end of the farm to the other herding the cattle together.

When he had rounded them up he pushed them far away out of the farm into an open space. He counted the cattle and discovered one was missing. Clint stayed in the rain looking for the missing cattle. He found it sitting by a tree. It was Ambala. All attempts by Clint to make it get up failed. Clint could not understand why. He tried to push Ambala up a few times but failed. Then it dawned on Clint that Ambala may be injured. He inspected Ambala and discovered it had gone lame. It must have injured itself in the stampede. Clint knew that there was nothing he could do for the injured cow. It hurt him to have to lose any. The herd was entrusted to his care and he wanted to give it back intact. He looked over at the herd; they had moved a small distance away and were grazing.

Clint sat down next to Ambala and thought about Alhaji. He wished Alhaji was around. Alhaji would have known what to do. Darkness was slowly descending. Clint decided to sleep there for the night. He knew that there was not much he could do again for the day. He sat beside Ambala, covered himself the best he could and lowered his hat down to his eyes. His clothes were soaking wet and he felt a little depressed. He watched the herd settle down one by one as the rain started to ease out just as quickly as it had come.

Clint stared at the herd, and talked to Ambala well into the night. Drops of rainwater continued to fall on his hat and onto his body. Clint thought of Alhaji. He missed Alhaji and he missed the gang. He did not know when his body resigned itself to the tiredness he felt. He fell asleep. He had an almost sleepless night and dreamt about Ambala throughout his sleep.

He woke up early, changed from his wet clothes and went to rouse the cattle with the stick Alhaji had given him. As he herded the cattle together he remembered the veterinary. He hoped the man there would be able to help him with Ambala. Ambala was looking very weak to Clint. The herd had started to move. They were led by Gala. It was as if they could read his mind. Clint went after the herd. It pained him to have to leave Ambala. Clint was almost becoming emotional. Clint pushed them faster than ever before, almost at a trot. They continued at this pace until both Clint and the herd were tired and had to slow down.

CHAPTER EIGHTEEN

The two Idele brothers cycling back from the farm almost ran over Alhaji laying on the footpath. They crashed into the bush to avoid him. The two brothers dismounted and went to examine the old man lying on the road. They did not recognize him. He could not possibly be from their area. Alhaji had tried to trace his way to the village. He could sense he had almost made it when he collapsed on the footpath. Edem Idele felt his heart. It was still beating.

"He is still alive, help me put him on the bike," he said.

They unloaded the vegetables and the foodstuffs they had harvested for the day, grabbed Alhaji and attempted to put him on the bike. Alhaji opened his eyes.

"Where am I?"

"You will be alright," answered Edem Idele

"Hold on here." He climbed the bicycle with Alhaji holding on to the handle bars then he turned to his younger brother.

"Bring the foodstuffs with you when you are coming."

Edem Idele pedaled away towards the village.

The two brothers had left very early in the morning to the farm. They were not expected back in the house just yet. Edem rode into the compound shouting for his other brothers to come out quickly.

"Effiong, John, the two of you help me take this man into the house."

The three of them carried Alhaji into the house. They put him on a mat while Effiong's wife prepared a bed. The brothers wanted to know what happened but Edem spoke to them with his eyes. They understood he would tell them later.

"Effiong go and get a doctor!" ordered Edem.

By the time Alhaji was carried again and placed on the bed, he was half-conscious.

Not long after he passed out. Effiong rode at top speed ringing the bicycle warning bell all the way to the only doctor in the village. At first Dr Ekanem was puzzled at the story Effiong had told him. After a few questions he could make out that his help was needed, as Effiong's brother Edem had ridden into the village with a strange man who was unconscious. Dr Ekanem collected his medical treatment bag and rode on his cycle with Effiong behind him, back to the Idele's compound.

At the Idele's compound there appeared to be a waiting reception for him. A small crowd of villagers had gathered at the Idele's doorsteps. The doctor was quickly rushed into the house and to the room where Alhaji was now lying on the bed unconscious. While Edem spoke quickly, narrating to the doctor how he came about the patient, Dr Ekanem went through a thorough physical examination of Alhaji Tijani. He explained to the anxious waiting family that Alhaji Tijani was suffering from acute malaria with very high fever and exhaustion. John the youngest of the Idele brothers went out to narrate to the curious villagers what was happening. Dr Ekanem gave

Alhaji two injections then prescribed some tablets with vitamins and iron to be given to him. The doctor gave strict instructions that Alhaji should be allowed to have a good rest for a few days. He explained that he would come in later to take a look at the patient but expected the patient to regain consciousness after some hours and then to go into deep sleep. Dr Ekanem ordered everybody out of the room, took his medical bag and set off for home.

When Mrs Idele saw that the family members were slow to react she took immediate control, shooing them out of the room to the outside door where she now drove the crowd of onlookers still milling around. Mrs. Idele explained what the Doctor had said and the crowd dispersed, murmuring and gossiping amongst themselves. New arrivals who met them on the way were quickly briefed on what had happened as this was the biggest news and happening in the village for a long time. Till now nobody could tell who Alhaji was and where he was coming from. But the unwritten law of the village community was to give hospitality to a stranger in need of help. They will find out the details of the stranger when he got better.

CHAPTER NINETEEN

Clint put the cattle on the move again. He was more careful now. He stayed in the front to make sure they did not enter the farmlands again. He was making good time as he put the cattle at a trot again. He must help Ambala. He sympathized with the farmers. The herds could easily spoil their crops. The hills were many. A signboard directed him to Atanu. He headed towards the hills. It took him time to reach the top. From the top he was sure he would see the veterinary office. He was right. Clint strolled down the slope, keeping the cattle in check. He drew back to make sure there were no strays and that all the cattle except Ambala were with him. He spotted the signboard to the veterinary office and pushed over there. The vet had been sleeping under the tree. He was woken by the cattle. He stood up and looked for the pusher but could not see anybody. Clint came up from the rear.

"Hey where do you think you are going?" The vet spoke, looking at Clint with suspicion.

"Come here!"

The vet looked Clint up and down.

"Are you the one with the cattle?" he asked.

"Yes," answered Clint.

"Where are your papers?"

Clint remembered that Alhaji had not given him any papers.

"I have no papers with me. The papers are with the owner."

"And where is the owner?"

The vet was becoming more skeptical.

"He fell ill on the way and I had to continue with the cattle to Lagos."

"Who are you?"

It dawned on Clint that the man may be suspecting he stole the cattle.

"I am Clint."

"Where are the other pushers? Sometimes there are more than two."

"I am the only other pusher. I had joined Alhaji on the way."

The vet was still suspicious. Clint then told the vet how he had left Igandu and joined Alhaji at Igara.

After more questions the vet was not convinced and decided to detain Clint.

"I think you better wait here. I can't let you go until I am convinced you didn't steal the cattle. This is a funny way to dress to push cattle. Go and sit over there. You will wait until the policeman comes."

The vet went across to the cattle to check them. He also wanted to see if there were any signs of the cattle having been stolen. While he was checking, Clint walked back to him. He explained what happened about Ambala. How he had to leave it behind. The vet explained that there was nothing he could do. He told Clint that before nightfall the people in the area would have killed it and divided up the meat. Clint shook his head and went to sit down. He was very sad at what he just heard, more so since he had told Ambala he would come back for him. It was a promise he could not fulfill.

The policeman was due back in the office in the evening just before the vet closed. Clint sat down feeling depressed. His mind would not leave Ambala.

The vet had gone back to the tree and was now resting. Clint pulled his hat over his head and was deep in thought. He was worried. He wondered if he would ever leave. He would have to explain everything to Alhaji. Clint suddenly realized he was tired. He still had plenty to do. Within a short time, Clint was asleep. He hadn't slept up to thirty minutes when he opened his eyes. A policeman was discussing with the vet.

"Well, they don't normally steal." The policeman assured the vet who was still suspicious.

"Only this one is dressed rather funny."

They both looked at Clint. The police officer motioned to Clint.

"Come over here."

Clint was a little apprehensive.

"How come you are alone with the cattle?"

Clint again narrated how he joined Alhaji from the beginning until Alhaji fell sick. He explained the instructions Alhaji gave him. He explained he did not know about the papers and Alhaji was too ill to remember.

"There is no point detaining you. I have looked at the herd and they are okay."

"Have you got money for the certificate?" asked the vet still looking at Clint's clothes.

Clint counted the money and handed it to him. The vet tore out the original of the certificate and handed it to Clint. They watched Clint stroll over to the cattle.

"Hey Jana hey!"

Clint and the cattle moved out. The police officer and the vet continued to stare at them. The vet shook his head.

"There is nothing we won't see nowadays."

The police officer nodded in agreement. Clint drove the cattle for a few hours before nightfall. Most of the day had gone. He had pushed for three hours and arrived at Oburu. He spotted the railway track. It was just as Alhaji had described it. Further down must be the water. Soon he found a suitable place to graze. Clint stopped for a rest. He decided to spend the night there and make an early start the next day. It was a chance for him to rest and gather himself.

"Gala! Tell the rest we will graze here for the night."

Clint checked all the cattle to make sure they were all right. Ever since losing Ambala, he checked the cattle regularly. He sat down and looked after them for some time then he went to gather some wood. He wanted to drink some warm lemon grass before he slept.

Alhaji had taught him how to know the different type of bushes and the different types of grass that could be of use to him on the journey. He had been amazed at the vastness of Alhaji's knowledge on life in general. He went in search of water. When Clint got to the water he poured water on his face to clear his head. Using his hat he scooped the water to drink. By the time he came back with the water, darkness had already come down. He lit the firewood and to his surprise the whole grass around him went up in flames. Clint ran for safety. The flames started to rise and spread. Clint immediately ran back to the fire trying to stop it but he could not.

The fire had caused the cattle to stampede once more. Clint raced through the fire forgetting his own safety. When he had cleared the fire he dropped his blanket, his bag, and his shoes. He went after the herd. The herd had run a long distance. Clint used the stick to try to bring them back together. Some had run into the bush and were hidden by the long grass and bushes while others had crossed back across the railway line. Clint slowly rounded them up. It took him almost four hours to complete the job. He pushed them to safety. The fire did not burn for too long before it died down. Only the very dry area had burnt.

Clint realized how lucky he was. He did not know the grass around that area had dried up and was likely to catch fire. Alhaji must have overlooked such likely occurrence hence his not having warned him. This was a lesson learnt. He went back and collected his blanket, bag and shoes.

Clint decided to sleep near the cattle to calm them down and keep his eyes on them. He decided to forego the lemon grass drink for the night and settled himself down watching the dying smoke. He sat thinking about what he had gone through. He thought of Alhaji. He remembered the gang and wondered how they would have coped if they had undertaken this journey. What would they be doing now? He wondered. It was a Thursday. On a Thursday night, they would surely go to the cinema.

Then Clint's mind went to Alhaji again. Clint silently hoped he would see Alhaji soon. He was sure Alhaji would be getting better by now. Clint spent most of the night thinking, going over his life, going over his adventure and wondering what the future will hold. He wondered what Lagos was like. Clint wrapped himself with blanket. He lowered his hat to his favorite position and leaned his head back against the tree. He watched the stars for a while and calculated his movement for the next day. Then he closed his eyes hoping to catch a little sleep.

In the morning Clint rose early, rinsed his face and went to rouse the herd. He felt he had lost so much time and if he continued in this way he would not make it to the head bridge on time. He didn't want to think or believe he would not make it to the bridge at Okuta. What would he tell Alhaji Tijani if he did not make it? He wondered how Alhaji was. He was sure Alhaji would make it to the bridge on time. Clint felt Alhaji was dogged and would not give up his journey. In no time he had the cattle moving at a trotting pace. Once in a while one would veer off from the rest. Clint would move quickly to put it into line running after or with the others. They maintained this pace until suddenly the herd veered out of their path and continued running. Clint moved fast trying to get them back on the route. He discovered they had been near a farm and the farmers had put a fence round their crops. Clint noticed that the herd was almost stampeding again. He raced after them. They were now running downhill. Clint did not know the hill was steep. The herd continued downhill, some stumbling while others could barely stand on their feet. Clint attempted to keep up with them but found it was not possible. The cattle started to scatter with some going a different route to the leader. Clint too fell down the hill. He tried to hold on to something to break his fall but could not. By the time he reached the bottom of the hill and had stopped rolling down he discovered he was covered with cuts and bruises. Clint got up immediately only to discover the herd had scattered and some had run very far before coming to a stop. Clint looked around. The vegetation was very sparse and he could see into the distance where some of the cattle were. Then he noticed one of the cattle lying down and obviously in pain. Clint went over to inspect it. He discovered it was Jali the wicked bull and one of its legs was broken. Clint talked to Jali trying to calm him.

He shifted him a little to make him more comfortable. Then he went off trying to round up the rest. The rounding up was not as easy as it looked since some had gone far. Clint found he had to push them all back to a spot where they can stay and graze while he went after those that were still scattered. He could only round them up one or two at a time because they were not all next to each other. When he had finished and counted the cattle he still found that two were missing. Clint searched everywhere for them until he found that they had run into a farm. To his relief the farmers were not around. He rounded them up. He pushed them at a trot back to the others. By the time the cattle had settled down, most of the day had gone again.

Clint pushed for a few hours more until he came to a suitable spot where he could rest and the cattle could graze again. He settled them down and went in search of some fruits to eat. He had run out of food and he was tired and hungry. Clint managed to collect some mangoes and coconut. He also saw a banana tree with lovely tempting and ripe bananas. He cut off the banana and carried all the fruits he could carry back to where he had picked out to rest. He put some in his bag and then went out to pick lemon grass to make himself lemon tea. He believed the tea would stop him from getting fever. After eating the fruits to his satisfaction, Clint relaxed leaning on a tree.

For some time he watched the cattle until tiredness and exhaustion started to take its toll. Clint spread his blanket on the ground and lay down. It had been a tiring day. Clint looked around. All was quiet. From where he lay he could see all the cattle and would be able to see anyone approaching. He was not put off by all the things that had been happening to him since he had to push the cattle alone. He felt faith was truly testing him in his desire to live the life of a cowboy. He felt his faith in himself was strong and he would pull through. He soon fell asleep. Towards the later part of the night he fell into a deep sleep.

CHAPTER TWENTY

Alhaji had spent 5 days in bed recuperating when he regained full consciousness. He was surprised to find himself lying on the bed. He looked around the room and from the pictures on the wall and the dressing table, he realized he was in a family house. In a short while, Effiong's wife Mrs Idele came in. She was surprised to see him conscious. She introduced herself. Mrs Idele explained to Alhaji how he had come to be in their house and the medical treatment he was given. Alhaji introduced himself and thanked her profusely. All offers by him to give money at least to offset the treatment were rebuffed by Mrs Idele. She went out and called the other members of the family. They came in to introduce themselves, happy to see that Alhaji was up and getting well again.

Within a short while, the news had spread to the village and those villagers that had not gone to the farm rushed over to have a glimpse of the stranger and to find out more about him. Alhaji was overwhelmed by their concern and interest. He told them more about himself and what he could remember happened before he passed out. Soon the news spread even to the farms that the stranger was a Dan Fulani and had regained consciousness. Those who could leave the farm did so to get a better look and hear firsthand how he came about coming to the village. Those who could not, postponed going to the Idele compound until when they closed. They made a mental note to close early.

Alhaji tried to explain why he had to leave soonest but the family and the villagers prevailed on him to wait for some more days until he had regained his strength fully. From that day, the room in which Alhaji was convalescing became like a mecca of sorts, as the villagers continued to troop in to see him, asking about his welfare, and bringing food and other gifts for him.

On the sixth day, Alhaji had woken up early. His thoughts were on Clint and his cattle. He worried for Clint's life and welfare and wondered how Clint could have managed. He tried to calculate where Clint should be on the road. He did not feel at ease. The urge for him to discharge himself and be on his way was too much to bear. He felt well and in good health. He felt strong. He felt he could not delay going much longer. He had regained all his strength. He considered his dilemma on how he could go without offending the Idele family. They had been so good to him. The whole village had been good to him but he had to start going. He had to find his way.

Mrs Idele came into the room with her husband and Edem. After the exchange of greetings they moved Alhaji and the bed to the window overlooking the court yard. Alhaji sat up in bed. The sun had already set and was shining into the room through the window. There was to be a marriage ceremony and Mrs Idele wanted him to see as much as he could, more especially the traditional musicians that would entertain the village. Alhaji had been very sick but now was much better but she still felt Alhaji needed more rest. The doctor had come in every day from the town and had been treating him. Mrs Idele had fussed over him the way they do with strangers, to make him feel welcome. She was now busy tucking in the bed cover.

"You sit up by the window and watch the ceremony. It is not every day we have a marriage in the village."

When Effiong and Edem had left, she told him all about the marriage ceremony. Since Alhaji opened his eyes and realized where he was, he had been speechless. Their hospitality had overwhelmed him. They had saved his life.

"I don't know how I can repay you. You have been so kind."

"The doctor says you will be well enough to go by tomorrow or anytime you wish." Mrs Idele told Alhaji to make him more cheerful.

That was good news for Alhaji. His mind went again to Clint and his cattle. Alhaji could not understand what had made him abandon Clint. The boy did not know the route. He knew nothing about cattle and anything could befall him on the road. He could be killed in any village for destroying the farmer's crops. Worse still, he was alone. Pushing cattle was a tough job for two experienced pushers, let alone one. Clint had no experience at all and Alhaji was worried. Alhaji realized he had been staring outside for some time without seeing anything. His mind had been far away. Mrs Idele had been staring at him.

"I am sorry, my mind was far away."

"I know. You must have a lot on your mind."

Alhaji remembered she had been telling him about a wedding in the village.

"Is it your daughter who's getting married?"

"No, it's my husband's brother's daughter, Edem's daughter. Edem is the brother that brought you here. They were coming from the farm with the yam they had harvested for today's ceremony."

Mrs Idele remembered that she would be playing a big role in the day's ceremony and she was going to be late.

"I have to go. We will be collecting the girl from the fattening room soon."

Alhaji was confused.

"Fattening room?" he asked.

"Oh we have to fatten her up and teach her the secrets of satisfying her husband.

We don't want the husband thinking she is not a complete woman. We will dress and beautify her."

"That's good," said Alhaji.

He was a very traditional man and he had learnt over the years to respect culture no matter which part of the country he was in.

"I must go. I am one of the Mothers of the Day. I will make sure they bring you something to eat. John will be in the house so just call out if you need anything."

As Mrs Idele left the room, Alhaji once again focused his attention on the courtyard. The sound of the music was filtering through to his room. The musicians soon appeared round the corner followed by the dancers. Excitement filled the air in anticipation of what was about to take place. The dancers and musicians were all dressed in colorful attire. The female dancers had dressed their hair elaborately with a large shiny comb through their hair. Alhaji could make out the bride and she looked beautiful. He regretted he would not be able to witness the wedding ceremony. He saw Mrs Idele cross the courtyard. Alhaji got out of bed and started to get dressed. His clothes had been washed for him.

"John!" He called out as he made his way to the sitting room.

John was surprised to see him fully dressed.

"Alhaji, you are not supposed to be out of bed."

"I have to go now. By my calculation my cattle are due at the bridge in Okuta in a day's time or two. I must be there to meet them."

"But the doctor said tomorrow!"

"Please, I did not want to worry Mr Idele and his wife. You have all been so good to me."

John did not know what to do or how to stop Alhaji. He asked Alhaji to let him at least tell Edem and Effiong that he was leaving but Alhaji pleaded with him not to trouble them. He explained that all he required was someone to travel with him to the bridgehead. He explained further that he wanted to give something to the person to bring back for the Idele family. John understood. He was much too junior to want to argue with Alhaji. He had wanted to go out when Alhaji called him back and asked him to keep it a secret between them.

"I understand," replied John. "You can trust me. I'll get you somebody."

Alhaji went back to the room and collected his bag. He came back into the sitting room to meet John and Akpan.

"Akpan will go with you. You will be ok. He is our cousin."

"Please thank my hosts for me and explain to them."

"No problem," replied John.

Alhaji thanked John and begged him again to explain to the Idele's his reason for going away. Alhaji and Akpan set out taking the road out of the village. The bride was being escorted around the courtyard and the wedding ceremony had begun.

CHAPTER TWENTY ONE

The tinkling sound was in his subconscious. Clint opened his eyes slowly. It took time for him to focus on what appeared to him like a mirage. In the distance was a group of Atilogu dancers about to do an early morning practice. They were walking towards him and chatting to themselves. They took their positions. Clint saw a performance of dance steps that looked like magic to him. He kept crawling nearer and nearer to the group. At first, an anthill had covered part of his view. He crawled to the side and watched the dancers until the leader of the group led them into the forest. Clint shook his head in amazement. He felt as if he had been dreaming. His head was heavy. This could not have been a dream. He could still hear the music as it went further and further away. He went over to the stream and rinsed his face then he walked over to the cattle.

"Gala, did you see that?"

The cattle were already beginning to understand his style. They got up.

"Hey Jana hey!" He shouted and they started to move.

He continued to relive the dance he had just seen wondering where they had come from and why he had not seen them earlier. Then he remembered that the meaning of the word Atilogu was spiritual. It meant "Is there magic in this." That dance was famous all over the country but he had never seen it close up like this and for free. The dance surely lived up to its name.

The steps were truly magical. Clint pushed the cattle out of the bush and onto the express road. The cars sped by. Some slowed down when they approached the herd. Some glanced at him as they passed. He could see the road stretching far into the distance. They were making good time. He was happy the dancers had woken him up. Now he was nearing the bridge. He knew that once he got to the bridge, the ordeal was over. Clint felt this was not the time to be weak. He had almost made it and he felt Alhaji would be proud of him. His mind again went to Lagos. The nearer he got to the bridge the more he thought of Lagos. What would he do in Lagos? He decided to leave that until he got there. He had heard so much about Lagos and had never been to a big city like that before.

After about four hours, he noticed more and more people were passing him on the road. He had entered the outskirts of the town. The traffic was getting heavier too. He walked in front of the cattle with the stick on his shoulder Dan Fulani style. He felt like posing. He put a swagger to his walk. He was feeling happy knowing he was almost there. He led the cattle down the high street. People stopped. People made way for them. He could hear some whispering to his hearing. He heard the word cowboy mentioned a few times. He enjoyed the attention he was getting. Those who were afraid of cattle ran for their safety. They only came out when the herd passed. The high street sloped down, and he could see the river and the bridge not too far in the distance. They went past the shops, by the market, through the low density residential area and finally through the ghetto by the river side. He remembered that the River Niger was to pass the town of Okuta to the ocean, and concluded that this must be the River Niger. Sometimes his cattle caused a lineup of cars to move very slowly. The cars crawled past the herd. At another time the traffic stopped completely. The herd also stopped. A few people cursed him. Some wound up their window glass as a protection against the horns of the cattle. A Good Samaritan took up the work of a traffic warden and directed the cars until the traffic moved again. Sometimes the blaring music from the loudspeakers placed practically on the road unnerved the cattle. Clint managed to calm them down and lead them on. At a field overgrown with grass, the cattle stopped to feed. Clint did not rush them. He knew they were hungry. He also knew they had made it.

He saw another herd grazing at the other end of the field and strolled over to the Dan Fulani to ask for directions to the head bridge. After taking note and exchanging information and discussion Clint strolled back to his herd. He sat on the grass with them and watched them graze. When he felt ready to move on he shouted.

"Hey Jana Hey!"

They all got up and continued their journey to the head bridge. The Dan Fulani had advised them not to attempt to go to the head bridge now as there was heavy go slow traffic caused by the luxury buses, transport buses, trailers, and private cars coming and going on the bridge. They would make it near impossible to reach the loading part of the bridge before darkness fell. He directed them where to graze and settle for the night and to head for the bridge early before the early morning traffic had built up again. Clint took the advice and headed to the field to rest for the night. He hardly slept that night. He felt good that he had almost reached the head bridge. He hoped Alhaji would be there. He wondered how he would find Dauda in the event that Alhaji was not there. Clint looked at the cattle and shook his head. Yes we made it together, he thought as he lowered his hat and tried again to sleep.

CHAPTER TWENTY TWO

Alhaji had got to the bridge ahead of Clint. He had met his son Dauda waiting with the trailer as pre-arranged. Dauda had been shocked to see him without the cattle. Alhaji explained what had happened, to Dauda. He also told him about Clint. All enquiries about Clint made by the two of them came to naught. Nobody had seen Clint or heard anything about him. Dauda had been a bit skeptical about Clint. The story his father had told him was almost unbelievable. He had offered to go towards the route of the cattle drive to see if he would see the boy but his father had told him to wait. Akpan had left to go back to the village. Alhaji had bought two cows from the cattle market in the town, hired a pick-up bus and sent him back with the cows and with his compliments to the Idele family. He promised he would be back to see the family when he had settled down and started his retirement.

Alhaji was impatient and anxious. He stared with his eyes glued on to the road leading to where the trailers load. For the rest of the day he had been restless. He walked up and down the head bridge asking questions. When he could no longer stand it he would make a small foray into the town with the hope of seeing Clint. He did not know they were less than thirty minutes apart. He came back to the head bridge dejected. Dauda did not know how to console his father and wondered who this Click was. His mind went through all possibilities about the cattle, including that Clint may have run away with the cattle. In the evening he tried to convince his father to have an early night, since by their calculations Clint should still come the next day. Try as he might Alhaji could not sleep. He worried more about Clint than the cattle. He was happy to see the morning light.

Alhaji said his prayers and prayed for Clint's safe arrival. After cleaning up, Dauda made tea with bread and egg for him but Alhaji could only take the tea. After his tea he did a short walk around the bridge with Dauda. He kept his eyes glued on the road to the head bridge. At first Alhaji was not sure until he squinted his eyes. There was a Dan Fulani coming and wearing cowboy clothes. It was Clint. Clint too had noticed the trailers but the sea of heads made it impossible for him to see Alhaji. A smile came to Alhaji's face. He was filled with joy and became emotional.

"There he is. Click, Click!" he shouted.

Dauda looked up the road and saw the cowboy leading the cattle towards the trailers. Before he could react, Alhaji had already started running shouting Clint's name in his own peculiar way. Dauda shook his head in disbelief. So it was true, he thought. Clint heard his name. The voice was unmistakable. He saw Alhaji weaving his way through the crowd running towards him. Tears came to Clint's eyes. He was so happy to see Alhaji. He ran towards him shouting. They both hugged each other. It was only when Dauda, who had been chasing his father arrived that Clint and Alhaji left each other.

"You made it!" shouted Alhaji.

"Thanks be to Allah."

"I was a little delayed, that's why I was late," answered Clint.

"You made it. Let's load up and head for Lagos in time for the market."

Alhaji turned to Dauda.

"This is Click. He made it. Click this is my son Dauda."

Clint and Dauda shook hands. Dauda was still looking at Clint and trying to make sense of what he was seeing. His father had talked so much about Clint in the short time they were waiting for him, but he never expected the shock of what he saw. He did not know what to think about the clothes.

"Dauda! Get the boys! Let's start loading. We will need the two trailers."

Clint was staring at Alhaji.

"Alhaji, how do you feel now?"

"I am fine. I am happy. I cannot begin to tell you. You have lived my dream for me. We have a lot to talk about and a lot to tell each other."

While Dauda went to get the cowhands Alhaji took Clint over to a shed where the market supervisors sit to rest from the sun. One of the supervisors, in respect for Alhaji Tijani's, age made way on the bench for them to sit down. Normally only the supervisors could use or sit in this shed. Alhaji did not waste time to start narrating what happened and how he found his way back to the head bridge. Clint told Alhaji about the two bulls he lost. He wanted to blame himself but Alhaji told him not to worry or blame himself. He explained that such things happened on a push and they were lucky not to have lost more. He praised Clint for his skill in bringing the cattle to the head bridge, after all, he explained it was Clint's first attempt at cattle pushing.

Clint felt more relaxed and then told Alhaji about his adventure. He told him about the vet and how they had forgotten the receipt. He told him how he lost Ambala and Jali. He explained how he used the stars to work out his route, his problem with the farmers and how he lost his way twice. When he had finished, Alhaji Tijani congratulated him once more. He praised him for successfully leading the cattle to the bridge, explaining that now their work was easier. They both stood up and Alhaji guided Clint to the trailers to watch the cattle being loaded. The cattle hands pushed the herd into the trailer with Dauda supervising. It took them quite some time to load all the cattle. Alhaji brought out Clint's gun.

"Click, here is your gun. You will want to wear it into Lagos."

Clint put his gun in its holster. He had almost forgotten about it. Alhaji put his hand around Clint's shoulders.

"Dauda, Click lets go. Dauda call the driver. We must get to Lagos on time."

Clint removed his boots from his neck. He excused himself from Alhaji and walked over to where he noticed a shoe cobbler. The cobblers usually walk around the market selling shoe slippers or repairing torn or worn leather slippers. Clint had the boy cobbler nail the loose heels back properly. He paid him and put his boots back on. He wanted to enter Lagos in style. The lead trailer could only take three passengers in front. Clint decided to ride hanging by the side. All entreaties by Alhaji and Dauda to get him to ride with the driver failed. He preferred to ride by the side. This was the way he had seen cowboys ride on wagons or on trains. With his gun he felt like a full cowboy again.

Alhaji turned to Clint as he hung by the side of the trailer.

"How do you say it in cowboy way when you want to move?"

Clint smiled and answered.

"Get 'em up, move 'em out. Giddy yup!"

Alhaji's attempt to repeat it sent everybody into laughter with Alhaji laughing the loudest.

Clint did not explain to them but the reason he had so wanted to ride by the side of the trailer was to get the feeling of riding shotgun. It had always looked exciting to him when he saw cowboys doing it on the stagecoaches. He was so happy he could afford to dream again. During the drive to Lagos, Clint lived some of his fantasies. He would jump into the trailer with the cattle. Sometimes he would come out and hang by the door of the trailer while it was moving to talk to Alhaji. Alhaji would laugh each time Clint came to the door shouting "Ya hoo!" and would caution him to be careful. Clint then went into a song he remembered from Rawhide.

Rolling rolling rolling
Keep 'em doggies rolling
Keep 'em doggies rolling
Rawhide.
Through rain and wind and weather
Hide bound for leather
Wishing my girl was by my side.
Through rain and wind and weather
My true love will be waiting
Waiting at the end of my ride.
Move 'em up. Get 'em up, move 'em up, get 'em up
Move 'em up. Get 'em up, Rawhide
Ride 'em in. Ride 'em out. Ride 'em in. Ride 'em out
Ride 'em in, Rawhide.

It did not matter to Clint that he did not know the words well. He sang it like that all the same. It was the way the song sounded to him and the way the gang and the crowd sang it in the hall. The singing was off key and it made Alhaji, Dauda and the driver to laugh. They laughed and laughed that at a point they tried to join Clint in the singing. They had been on the road for most of the day before the euphoria of his achievement started to wear out.

It was also beginning to get dark. Clint climbed in once more with the cattle and made some space for himself. He pulled his hat down over his eyes and started to sing the theme song to Rawhide once more. He sang to himself in a low voice until the song faded off. Clint sighed. I did it, he thought. Yes I did it. Clint's head bent a little as he gave way to tiredness and fell asleep.

Alhaji too was now relaxed. The tiredness had caught up with both of them. Alhaji put his head on Dauda's shoulder. He too went to sleep. The trailer made its way through the night to Lagos.

CHAPTER TWENTY THREE

The cattle herd was restless and were trying to move around inside the trailer. Clint woke up to the early morning sunshine. He guessed they were in Lagos. He could see the Lagos skyline of skyscrapers in the distance. He had never seen such buildings before nor had he seen such structures as the flyover bridges. He climbed to the side of the trailer to Alhaji. He greeted Alhaji, Dauda and the driver. They greeted him too.

"Ah, Click, you are up. This is Lagos."

"I have never seen anything like it before."

Alhaji laughed. He laughed more often now.

"Alhaji, the cattle are restless," explained Clint.

"Well that's because we are almost there. When the cattle are going to market, they sense they are going to die. This makes them restless."

"What's the market in a great city like this like?"

"Ah, when we get to the market, it is going to be another battle. The bargaining is very difficult, if you want best prices for your cattle."

They spoke for a little while with Clint asking more questions, then Clint went back to stand in the trailer with the cattle, feasting his eyes on Lagos. To Clint, Lagos looked an exciting place. There were tarred roads everywhere. Igandu had only one tarred road going through the center of the town and no flyover bridges. Lagos looked big and crowded. People were everywhere. There was water everywhere too.

Inside the town, the water separated some parts

of the town from other parts. There were many bridges as the city was an island. Markets were everywhere too. People were selling on the roads, in the shops and in the market place. Clint felt there were no bungalows in Lagos. Every house was decked, some climbing into the sky. There were many cars and lorries on the roads. Clint did not realize his mouth was open as he looked at Lagos with awe. He wished the gang were with him in Lagos to see how the city was. They had sometimes talked about Lagos but what he saw now was far different from what they thought. He wondered how he was going to survive in this town. What was he going to do? Maybe Alhaji would help him to get a job with another pusher. Could he push cattle for a living? He had now experienced it. The life of a cowboy was tough. With the money he had and maybe Alhaji would give him some money, he should be able to survive for a few days or weeks, depending on how expensive it was in Lagos.

They drove alongside an expanse of open land and what seemed like the cattle market in the distance. From where he stood in the trailer, Clint could see that the market was fenced with demarcations inside. There were many cattle herds in the market. The cattle herds were kept in groups in their enclosure. Clint could see people inspecting the cattle. The trailer drove into the cattle depot. Cowhands rushed at them running with the trailer and hoping they would be able to get some work with the owner. Ibrahim spotted the trailer and pointed at it for his mother to see.

Fati shouted and ran with Ibrahim towards the trailer. Alhaji and Dauda alighted and embraced them. Fati was all over her husband, petting him and asking about his health and wellbeing.

Clint had jumped down and was standing beside the trailer. The market was filled with people. Ibrahim turned to his father.

"I have a buyer ready and waiting. Let's go and see him. Dauda you take care of the unloading."

Ibrahim and Fati led Alhaji away. Dauda started to organize the cowhands. He took control of offloading the herd leading them to the enclosure where they would be kept. Clint found himself standing alone. He seemed to have been forgotten. He looked over to where Alhaji was. Alhaji was busy discussing and bargaining. Clint could tell by the way he was gesticulating. Clint felt alone. He thought of the herd and felt bad that they would be slaughtered. They had become part of him. He thought of Gala. Still he was a cowboy. Clint adjusted his hat and his gun and walked away. He could not afford to be emotional about them. Alhaji was home. Maybe he had forgotten him. It was only natural. Maybe later he would come back to see if Alhaji could give him some money and to say goodbye. He walked through the market, attracting glances from here and there. The trip had been worth it. He was happy that he took the decision to join a cattle push. He had achieved the impossible. If only Rogers and the gang were around. He had an unbelievable tale to tell.

Clint had never seen so many people and cattle

in one place. He saw the cattle pushers with a different eye now. It was a shame the cattle were going to be slaughtered. If only Gala could be saved. Gala deserved as much credit for the success of the push as he did, Clint thought. There were so many cattle at the market, most of them must have come by trailer. But there were still a few that came on foot. He looked at the cattle pushers. He felt they deserved more credit and respect. They truly were the real cowboys. He wondered if any of them knew what he had done, to push cattle from Kafanchan to Lagos. This was surely a journey of a lifetime. Clint walked round the market. There were hawkers everywhere with all kinds of goods. There was, bread, rice, milk and local medicines for all types of illnesses. There were food vendors, grilled meat known as suya, was being grilled on the fire. The noise of the market was loud. Clint enjoyed the euphoria of arriving in Lagos. Some of the cattle were lying around. Some were grazing. The floor was very muddy. Some cattle were being led to slaughter. But amidst all the achievement, Clint felt lonely.

He walked out of the market and started trekking towards the city of Lagos. He walked atop the small bridge linking the market with the city and found himself immersed in the hustle and bustle that was Lagos. Stalls were placed on the roads sometimes making it difficult for cars to pass. People dressed differently in Lagos compared to Igandu. There were sky scrapers everywhere, some with walls that seem to be

made of glass. The shops were lit with colored lights and some roads had statues and water fountains. He marveled at the different things for sale. The buildings were so different from the dilapidated buildings he was used to. Motor cars of different makes were passing by. Everything was different. The shops had things he had never seen before. He wondered when he would ever have enough money to buy some of those things. Everywhere there were crowds. They must all live somewhere. Where could they all be going? he asked himself. Everything was new. Even with all these, he felt alone. He knew nobody. He wondered why Alhaji had forgotten about him. Well, he thought, he was just a young man playing at cowboys.

When he collects his money from Alhaji, he would then decide what to do. The further he went down the high street, the more glances he got. He put a strut to his walk. They should know he was a cowboy. They should know what he had achieved. He walked the length of Kingsway Stores marveling at the goods displayed at the windows. He walked through the glass door. The size of the shop was more than twenty times bigger than the biggest shop in Igandu. The toy trains in the window had attracted him inside. He marveled at the clothes on display. The store attendants did not know what to make of him. They watched him closely. Clint noticed that two women in the store were staring at him. He tilted his hat and greeted them cowboy style.

"Howdy ma'am."

The ladies smiled at him. Clint heard the fat, light complexioned one ask the other what he had said. The other woman had replied that she heard something about an "Imam" a Muslim priest. Clint smiled and continued walking and inspecting the shelves. There were shelves filled with food stuffs. There were rows and rows of tinned and packaged foods, electronic goods, a music corner with the sound turned low, television sets etc. He resisted the temptation to buy something. He did not have much money and he wanted to wait until he was sure of what he wanted to do. He definitely may have to live on the little money he had in his pocket until he found a job.

At the other end of the shelf, a little white boy of about six-years old had noticed Clint. The boy was dressed in a child's cowboy outfit with Roy Rogers written on the waistcoat. Clint looked up and was surprised to see the boy standing in the middle of the passageway. The boy stood with his legs spread apart, cowboy style, ready for the gun duel. It was the cowboy's way of knowing who was the fastest on the draw and the toughest. It was a challenge. Clint's ego and reputation was at stake. He could not back out. This was the final proof of being a cowboy. This silent challenge of who could draw the gun out first from the holster. Everything he had lived for all these years depended on this action. To the boy, it was playing at cowboys. Clint did not see it that way. This was the first time he had been challenged to the draw by a stranger, and a white boy for that matter. Being a white boy made it more real. He had never seen a white boy in real life before. He had never seen one in a cowboy outfit. He just had to draw against him. This was the way it was in films. This was the way cowboys were. This was real.

Clint walked the way he had seen Clint Eastwood do it in "First full of dollars." He threw his blanket over his shoulder to expose his gun more. He moved his mouth as if he had a thin cigar there. Then he squinted his eyes. The boy's walk reminded him of Wyatt Earp in "Gunfight at OK Coral." Shoppers noticed what was about to happen and began to make room for the cowboys. The boy's mother turned to her companion.

"Oh, look! There's another cowboy over there."

This confirmed to Clint that the show down was real. Clint and the boy stared at each other waiting for who would make the first move. The shoppers were curious to know who would win. The whole shop was silent as the shoppers made a form of semi-circle around the two cowboys. The cashier nervously looked at the foreman. The store's foreman moved from one of the shelves to stop them but the manager had reached him and put a restraining hand on him. He told the foreman in a low tone to leave them.

The little boy drew first and had his gun out of his holster before Clint could draw. The whole store started clapping. The ceiling started to spin around Clint. He could not believe it. He had been beaten to the draw by the white boy in the presence of so many people. The shame was too much for him. Everything he had been all these years disintegrated right in front of his eyes. He felt faint. Sweat was showing on his face. He needed some air. Clint staggered out of the store in a daze. He took in gulps of fresh air wondering what the rest of the gang would say. What could he tell them? In all this time he had believed so much in himself, in being tough, in being a cowboy. For the first time in his life, he felt more alone than he had ever felt before. He could not get over the shame. He could not look people in the eye.

CHAPTER TWENTY FOUR

Alhaji was looking around. He could not see Clint. He turned to Ibrahim.

"Where is Click?"

Ibrahim had not been introduced to Clint and did not really understand his father. He made a sign to show his father he did not really understand him. Alhaji repeated the question.

"Click, he came in on the trailer with me."

Ibrahim turned to Dauda.

"Dauda, where is Click?"

Dauda shook his shoulders too to show he did not know where Clint was. Alhaji became worried.

"Two of you go and find him!" he ordered.

"Where will we find him?" asked Ibrahim.

"Find him. He is in Lagos somewhere. Bring him to the house." He instructed.

"But how will we recognize him?" Ibrahim asked again.

"He is a cowboy. How many cowboys are there in Lagos?" asked Alhaji.

"Take the car. Don't come back without him."

Ibrahim knew that his father's instructions had to be obeyed although he could not make head nor tail out of what his father was saying. He had not seen any cowboy when the trailer had arrived.

"What is his name again?" he asked once more to be sure he got it right.

Alhaji was now impatient and answered sharply.

"Click, Click!"

Ibrahim kept muttering to himself and repeating the name.

"Click, Click."

He turned to Dauda.

"Let's go and find him. Click, Click!" he shouted.

Dauda too started to shout "Click, Click!"

Soon the whole market was shouting "Click, Click!"

Everybody took up the shout. Alhaji was speechless. He did not know what to say. He was fed up. Dauda and Ibrahim went to the car and took off to search for Clint leaving behind a big crowd of people shouting,

"Click!"

After searching half the center of Lagos, they spotted Clint leaning on a lamp post with his hat in his hands and staring into the distance.

"That's him over there!" shouted Dauda.

The car pulled up beside Clint.

"You must be Click." said Ibrahim.

Clint's mind was far away deep in thought, he did not answer.

"Please! Alhaji wants to see you," continued Ibrahim.

Clint still remained silent. He had not even acknowledged their presence. After waiting for some time for an answer and none was forthcoming, Dauda decide to plead with Clint.

"Click, please! Father says we should not come back without you."

Clint looked down at the car and recognized Dauda and Ibrahim. Ibrahim knew he could not go back to his father without Clint, he too pleaded.

"Please the whole market is in confusion looking for you. Please come, Alhaji wants to see you."

"Where is Alhaji?" Clint asked at long last.

"He has gone to the house."

Clint put on his hat and hesitated.

"He has gone to the house. Please enter the car," continued Ibrahim to reassure him. Dauda came down from the car and opened the back door. Clint adjusted his hat down to his eyes and entered the car.

The car sped off to the house. All the time Clint was in the car he did not notice the luxury of Alhaji Tijani's Mercedes car. He was looking outside the window but was seeing nothing. Clint's mind relived the draw at the store. The more he saw it in his mind's eye the more depressed he became. He tried to console himself that he had made it to Lagos. It didn't work. He asked to no one in particular in his mind why this should happen to him here in Lagos. There was no answer. The car cruised on to the Eko flyover bridge, over the water flowing to the ocean. They entered the main Lagos Island on their way to the highbrow residential area known as Victoria Island where Alhaji also had a house.

They passed the beach known as the Bar beach. The sound of the waves finally attracted Clint's attention. He watched the waves as they rose and flowed towards the beach. Clint stared in disbelief as he saw people jump into the waves.

They were submerged by the waves and they floated up again. The beach was so big. Clint had never seen a beach before. The car cruised down Ahmadu Bello way and then into Alhaji Tijani's compound.

CHAPTER TWENTY FIVE

Alhaji was sitting on the settee with Fati his wife and his two daughters fussing over him when Clint and his sons entered the sitting room. Clint was feeling a little better. He was surprised at Alhaji's house. It was so big and luxurious. The house was painted all white with marble floors. Paintings and carvings hung all over the walls. A painting of a cattle pusher on a push briefly caught Clint's eye. Clint was a little nervous. He never knew Alhaji was such a rich man. Alhaji was bigger than Clint thought. He had never entered such a house before. Alhaji got up, went to Clint and put his hand on Clint's shoulder.

"Click, why did you go away like that? I have been looking for you. You've met my son Ibrahim and you know Dauda before. This is my wife Fati and these are my daughters, Aminatu and Hauwa."

Alhaji turned to Clint again.

"This is Click, I owe him everything."

They all exchanged greetings. The greetings lasted for more than five minutes, the African way. Clint had a brief exchange of looks with Aminatu.

Alhaji Tijani had been narrating the story of their journey to his wife Fati and his daughters right from the market place. He had talked so much about Clint that they had looked forward to meeting this young cowboy their father was so proud of. He had discussed the issue of offering Clint a job. Fati did not object but left the decision to him. She always felt he knew best. Alhaji had changed into a white kaftan while his wife Fati was dressed in a flowing gown. She was beautiful. The house looked so clean. Alhaji's daughters were whispering to themselves and glancing at Clint.

"Click!" Alhaji called him again in his own way.

"I want you to work for me. If you agree, I will be most happy and I will pay you well."

"Do you want me as a pusher?" Clint asked.

"No, not as a pusher," replied Alhaji.

"I am no more a cowboy." Clint spoke those words with a little hint of sadness in his voice.

"No, not as a cowboy. I want you to be my personal assistant."

Clint was silent. This may be the next most important decision of his life. The first was to have gone on this journey. But he knew Alhaji wanted his answer immediately. Alhaji was a nice man and he had come to like him very much. Alhaji looked at Clint and smiled to give him a little encouragement for his answer. Clint looked at Fati, she smiled at him. Then he looked at Aminatu and she shied away from his look but he had seen a little twinge of hope in her eyes and a little smile. Clint looked towards Ibrahim and Dauda but they were not paying attention. They were talking to themselves. He turned to Alhaji, smiled and nodded in acceptance.

"Good, good," said Alhaji.

"Aminatu show Click to the guest room. I have brought some clothes for you. I know you will want to bath and change, and then we will have some food."

Clint took off his hat and followed Aminatu to the room. Aminatu had been curious at the name "Click" since her father started to tell them about him. She could not resist asking him.

"Your name is Click?"

Clint looked at her and smiled. She was a very beautiful girl. He decided he was no more a cowboy. He will answer his real name from now. Clint looked at her trying to catch her eyes but she shied away.

"My name is Ahmed," he replied.